MY SOUL TO TAKE

USA TODAY BESTSELLING AUTHOR
ERIN BEDFORD

My Soul To Take © 2020 Embrace the Fantasy Publishing, LLC

All rights reserved under the International and Pan-American Copyright Conventions. No part of this book may be reproduced or transmitted in any form or by any means, electronic or mechanical, including photocopying, recording, or by any information storage and retrieval system, without permission in writing from the publisher.

This is a work of fiction. Names, places, characters and incidents are either the product of the author's imagination or are used fictitiously, and any resemblance to any actual persons, living or dead, organizations, events or locales is entirely coincidental.

Warning: the unauthorized reproduction or distribution of this copyrighted work is illegal. Criminal copyright infringement, including infringement without monetary gain, is investigated by the FBI and is punishable by up to 5 years in prison and a fine of $250,000.

Cover Design By: Moonstruck Cover Design and Photography http://moonstruckcoverdesign.com/

Interior Design: Embrace the Fantasy Publishing, LLC

Also by Erin Bedford

The Underground Series
Chasing Rabbits
Chasing Cats
Chasing Princes
Chasing Shadows
Chasing Hearts
The Crimes of Alice
Hatter's Heart
Cheshire's Smile

The Mary Wiles Chronicles
Marked by Hell
Bound by Hell
Deceived by Hell
Tempted by Hell

Starcrossed Dragons
Riding Lightning
Grinding Frost
Swallowing Fire
Pounding Earth

The Crimson Fold
Until Midnight
Until Dawn
Until Sunset

Curse of the Fairy Tales
Rapunzel Untamed
Rapunzel Unveiled
Rapunzel Unchained

Her Angels
Heaven's Embrace
Heaven's A Beach
Heaven's Most Wanted

House of Durand
Indebted to the Vampires
Wanted by the Vampires
Protected by the Vampires
Embrace of the Vampires
Tempted by the Butler
Loved by the Vampires
Huntress of the Vampires

Academy of Witches
Witching On A Star
As You Witch
Witch You Were Here
Just Witch It
Summer Witchin'

Children of the Fallen
Death In Her Eyes
Fire In Her Blood

House of Van Helsing
Her Cross To Bear

Fairy Tale Bad Boys
Beauty and the Hunter
Wendy's Pirate
More Than Gold

New Orleans After Midnight
Vampire CEO
Werewolf at Midnight

The Beast of the Fae Court
Granting Her Wish

Dedication

For my dad.
You drive me crazy every day but I wouldn't
trade you for anyone else.

P.S. Don't read this book!

Chapter 1

THE DAY I BURIED my dad, my best friend and confidant, was a miserable day indeed. Not that you could tell by the clear, sunny sky above us as the priest intoned my father's last rites.

I wasn't unfamiliar with loss. I'd lost my mother when I was eleven to breast cancer, so it seemed fitting I'd lose my dad ten years later. Except, this time, it was someone else who took my dad from me, not some sickness we could blame then say there was nothing we could do about it.

No. A distracted driver swerved into my dad's lane, killing them both and hurting a handful of other people. There wasn't even someone for me to be angry at! I didn't even get the satisfaction of seeing the asshole go to prison.

Peyton Rider. Pfft. What a name!

The preppy frat boy from Richmond College had a black, lifted pickup truck with a blue streak down the side. By the time the emergency crew arrived, the beautiful truck his rich parents had probably bought was nothing more than scrap metal.

My dad's little blue Fiat didn't stand a chance. At least the bastard went down with him. It was a bitter pill to swallow either way.

"Now, Gregory's daughter, Braxton, would like to say some words." The priest, a portly, older man with tiny glasses perched on his nose, gestured for me to come forward.

Standing from my seat next to Aunt Christine, I breathed deeply, my fingers curled into fists at my sides. *It's okay, Brax. You can do this. Don't cry. Don't cry.*

Pulling on the ends of my dirty blonde hair, I chanted my mantra all the way to the front of my dad's grave, my kitten heels sinking into the soggy grass beneath my feet. I pulled my index cards from the pocket of my black dress pants— the only article of clothing I had in the color—and gripped them tightly in my hands until the paper bit into my skin. Public speaking wasn't my area of expertise, I preferred online interaction, but this was for my dad. I could and would do anything for him.

"My dad, Gregory Clay, is—I mean, was—the best dad a girl could possibly ask for." A man from my dad's job coughed into his hand, interrupting my concentration. "He knew just what to say when I was having a bad day, and the right way to threaten bodily harm to anyone who broke my heart." I smiled slightly as the crowd chuckled. I stared down at my cards, struggling to get the words out. "He never said a bad word about anyone...unless they were downing his favorite team." I looked up and jokingly pumped a fist in the air. "Go Seahawks!"

My lips tugged down when no one responded in kind. Licking my lips, I shuffled my cards, my eyes jerking down to them and then back up to the group of somber people—a combination of my dad's work friends and our family. My Aunt Christine gave me an encouraging thumbs-up. Taking a deep breath, I closed my eyes then opened them again, my gaze landing on a stranger standing at the edge of the crowd.

A man about my age, or so it seemed from this distance, wearing a letterman's jacket and a tight frown. His sandy blond hair hung shaggily over his eyes as he shoved his hands deeper into the pockets of his jeans. I didn't recognize him as anyone I knew, and wondered how he might have known my dad.

A throat cleared.

I shook my head, turning my attention back to my index cards. "Uh, my dad, he, uh, he was one of a kind, and after Mom died, he really stepped up. I couldn't have asked for another dad like him." My jaw tightened and my hands closed firmly around the paper, crushing them. "And he didn't deserve to die like he did." I cursed under my breath. "He deserved...he deserved better." I ended lamely, dropping my clenched fists to my sides, my gaze on the ground where they were about to lower my dad's coffin into.

Six feet of dirt. That was where my dad would live from now on. In the dark and cold, all alone forever. I'd never hear his voice again. Hear him yell and slam the football down on the ground from the other side of the house when his team scored.

Tears burned in my eyes and I didn't fight them.

It wasn't fair. It just wasn't fair.

"Thank you, Braxton." The priest placed a hand on my back and gave me an awkward pat before nudging me gently forward.

I swiped a hand across my face and headed back to my seat. For some reason, my eyes drifted to where the letterman jacket guy had been, but he was gone. Putting it out of my mind, I sat beside Aunt Christine and let her wrap her arm around me. I leaned into her embrace. Her black, long-sleeved dress smelled of the expensive perfume she always wore, something French I couldn't pronounce, but it made me feel better. It was something familiar in this depressing place.

Aunt Christine was my dad's twin. However, while he had been tall and built like a mob boss, something we always joked about, Aunt Christine was petite with freckles all over her pale skin. The only things they had in common were the dirty blond of their hair and their light brown eyes. Two features I'd inherited as well. Thankfully, my build leaned more toward Aunt Christine's and not Dad's. I couldn't imagine trying to pull my tube top on over shoulders that big.

A small giggle escaped me.

"You okay, Brax?" Aunt Christine whispered, leaning toward my ear as the priest finished saying my dad's last rites.

I nodded and rubbed my face, knowing I probably looked like a drowned rat but not caring. The only person here that even cared about me was Aunt Christine, the rest could just go to hell.

Standing, I took the rose my cousin Billy had passed out to everyone closely related to Dad. As I approached the coffin, my hands shook and my knees threatened to give out on me. The mahogany coffin shined beneath the sunny sky, the bundle of white roses sitting on top only hiding what sat beneath the lid.

I never even got to see him one last time. The officer who came to my door told me that he

MY SOUL TO TAKE

suffered serious damage when that monster of a truck slammed into him. There wasn't enough of him left in one piece for me to identify. They had to use his dental records to get an ID on him just so they knew who to notify.

When they had informed me, I'd begged them to let me see him. I didn't care how messed up he was. I wanted, no, *needed* to see him. A social worker from the police station had to sit with me until Aunt Christine came to console me.

"Your dad wouldn't want your last memory of him to be that way," Aunt Christine had told me, and she'd been right. I didn't want to remember my dad like that.

I wanted to remember him leaving the house, laughing and joking about getting to the store before all the dogs got away. He was such a nerd. Like hot dogs could run away.

Shaking my head, I clutched the rose to my chest and smiled through my blurring vision before taking the final step forward. I placed the rose on the casket and rested my hand on the wood surface for a brief second. "Bye, Dad."

I moved to the side as I waited for my aunt and everyone else to get through the line. Some said nothing, others said a few words, and one woman from the grocery store threw herself onto the coffin and howled like a banshee. Dad said she gave him her store discount every time he went. I always kind of thought she had a thing for him. Looks like I was right.

Aunt Christine shook her head and smiled, placing her hand on my shoulder. "Come on, let's get you home. I hope you like casserole, because we're going to be eating it for weeks to come."

I groaned and followed her to the car. On the way, we passed by a caretaker clearing out some dead flowers. Giving him a polite nod, I turned away from him only to see that guy again.

He was standing off to one side, not talking to anyone, and no one even paid him any mind as they walked to their cars. Frowning, I took a step toward him.

"Hey, young lady." A hand touched my elbow, and I shifted around to see the caretaker. He was an elderly man with a receding hairline and more wrinkles than not, but his eyes were kind and gentle as he stared down at me.

"Yes?"

Dropping his spotted, wrinkled hand, the caretaker offered it to me in greeting. "I'm Edgar. I'm in charge of these grounds."

Not sure why he wanted to talk to me, I shook his hand with uncertainty. "Nice to meet you, I'm Braxton."

He chuckled, which turned into a cough. Releasing my hand, he pulled a handkerchief from the pocket of his pleated, sage-colored pants. "I apologize. I'm sure you're wondering why I stopped you, but you see, I'm looking for someone who can work the night shift. I'm getting too old to stay up all night." He chuckled and pounded his chest. "Not like you youngins."

"Okay," I drawled out, stupefied by his explanation.

"Anyway, I had a college kid helping me out during the weekends, but sadly..." He paused, a morose look crossing over his features. "He passed away a few months ago and I haven't been able to find anyone to replace him."

"I'm sorry for your loss." The words came out robotic, something I was sure I was going to have repeated to me in length over the next few days.

He waved me off. "My point is, you look about his age and I was just wondering...do you need a job?"

Taken aback, my brows furrowed together. "Excuse me?"

Edgar whipped his head back and forth rapidly. "Not that I'm saying you look like you need one, but I just..." He sighed and scratched the back of his head. "I'm desperate." An awkward silence filled the space between us, and then by some miracle Aunt Christine called for me just then.

"I'm really sorry." I stepped away from him. "But I have to go."

Digging into his pocket, Edgar pulled out a card and handed it to me. "Think about it. It would only be on the weekends, the pay is really good, and you get dental." He gave me a perfectly white toothed smile, and I couldn't tell if they were dentures or not.

I reluctantly accepted the card and tucked it into my pocket with a curt nod. "I will. Thank you."

Hurrying away from him as quickly as I could, I ducked into Aunt Christine's car. Shutting the door, I took one last look out the window at my dad's final resting place. If I worked there, I could see him all the time. Or at least be near him.

I shook my head and huffed a laugh. What was I thinking? Work at a cemetery? I wasn't that hard up for money.

Dad's life insurance had been enough to cover his funeral and the rest of his debt, leaving me a substantial sum that would last me for a while. Although, I didn't really care about giving up my weekends, since I didn't party with the rest of the students at my Hill Valley College—a small four-year college that was a far cry from Richmond.

Thinking of the college that douchebag Peyton attended made my hackles rise. Crossing my arms snuggly against my chest, I glared out the window. Did they bury him here as well? If they did, I needed to buy some eggs to throw at his grave. Immature, yes. But it would make me feel better. I hoped.

"What did Mr. Homing want?"

My aunt's voice interrupted my seething. I sat up and dropped my arms, pulling the card out of my pocket. "Nothing really. Just wanted to see if I wanted a job."

"Hmm. Did you take it?" Aunt Christine glanced over at me briefly before turning her attention back to the road.

I shrugged. "No. I don't know. I said I'd think about it."

Aunt Christine nodded in understanding. "Well, take some advice from someone a little bit older than you." She paused and winked. "Only a little bit. Save all the money you can. Your financial aid might be taking care of your tuition now, but things change, and you'll want a good nest egg to help you when that time comes." She took a deep breath and a soft smile covered her lips. "Besides, the less time you spend all alone in that big house, the better I'll feel."

I slumped in my seat. "Yeah. I guess. But a cemetery? Isn't that a bit...I don't know...morbid?"

Chuckling, Aunt Christine nudged me with her elbow. "Hey, we're all a bit morbid every now and again. Think of it as therapy. A chance to get closure." She shrugged a shoulder. "And who knows, you might like it. Maybe you'll actually pick a major."

"Pfft. Doubt it." I'd been in college for two years now and was nowhere near close to figuring out what I wanted to major in. I'd burnt out on electives and core classes. I knew a handful of nonsense about art history and more than I wanted to know about Egyptian hieroglyphs. Yep, I went through the phase of wanting to be an archeologist. We all did at one point, I figured. But digging in the dirt all the time was so not for me.

Maybe Aunt Christine was right. Maybe working at the cemetery would be just what I needed. Besides, it was only on the weekends. How hard could it be?

Chapter 2

OPENING THE FRIDGE, I scanned over the leftovers from the wake. My Aunt Christine hadn't been kidding about casseroles. I had tuna casserole, potato casserole, and even green bean casserole. I had noodle casserole up the ass. The plus side was, I didn't have to worry about finding something to eat. The negative was that all that casserole was going to my hips.

It'd been a week since the funeral. Since my world was turned upside down. It hadn't gotten any easier. There were nights I cried myself to sleep. Other nights, I stayed up just to look at his things. I wrapped myself in his shirts, inhaling his scent. Old Spice aftershave and motor oil. I always joked with him that he wasn't going to attract any women with that combination.

He'd just laugh as he worked on his 1965 Pontiac GTO. "Why do I need a woman? I have all the women I need with you and old Sherly here." He would stroke the canary yellow hood of the car like it was a woman's body. At the time, it made me want to puke, but now I just smiled in remembrance, tears forming in my eyes as I stared into the fridge.

Sighing, I shut the door and turned away from it. I couldn't stomach another casserole tonight. I had to get out of the house.

Since I didn't have a car of my own, I usually borrowed Dad's, but since the Fiat was a hunk of metal in the junkyard, all that was left was the Pontiac. Something he would have never let me drive if he was alive. Guess it didn't matter now.

Grabbing the keys off the hook, I slipped my tennis shoes on and headed out the back door. I pushed the button for the garage door and watched as it slowly lifted, revealing Dad's prized convertible. My chest tightened and I almost just said fuck it. I could down another plate of casserole tonight, but my aunt's words came back to me.

"You need to keep busy. Don't lock yourself away in this house. You'll waste away in your grief."

I'd promised I wouldn't turn into a hermit, but since I hadn't gone to class all week, I also hadn't left the house. The fact that I'd remembered to shower at all was amazing, let alone being able

MY SOUL TO TAKE

to face any of my friends or teachers. I was probably missing some vital schoolwork, but now, I couldn't find a shit to give.

I climbed into the driver's seat, having to push the seat up to fit my short legs. I adjusted the mirrors and cranked the ignition. It purred like a dream and eased out of the garage without a hitch. Pulling out into the street, I drove carefully, praying I didn't fuck this up. Couldn't lose one of the only things I had left of my dad the first day out.

The radio played some classic rock from the eighties, something my dad loved to blast at the risk of busted eardrums, but I couldn't bring myself to change the channel. My finger tapped on the steering wheel as I made my way to the local burger place. Except when I got there, several of my friends from school were hanging out in the front.

I grimaced. I might be able to get out of the house for some food, but I wasn't up to facing them just yet. All the questions, condolences, and attempts to cheer me up...I just couldn't play pretend today.

Dipping my head down in the car, I inched around the restaurant, aiming for the drive-thru. If I was lucky, I could get my food and get out of there before anyone spotted me.

"Can I take your order?" the staticky voice asked through the speaker on the clown shaped order box.

"Can I get two number fives, medium with a sweet tea to drink?" I spouted off without thinking.

"And what to drink with the other one?"

"Other one?" I repeated, and then realized I'd ordered two number fives, not one. It was what my dad and I always ordered. But he wasn't here. My mind drifted to the headstone sitting in the cemetery all alone in the dark.

"Ma'am?" the staticky voice prompted with an impatient tone.

Licking my lips, I hurriedly replied, "Uh, yeah. Sweet tea too. Thanks."

I drove around the building, paid at the window, and took my food, setting it in the passenger seat. As I was leaving, I forgot to duck until a voice called my name. Wincing at being caught, I forced a smile onto my face and slowed the car to a stop. "Mandy, hey."

"Brax! How are you? We've missed you at school." Mandy tossed her blonde hair over her shoulder, looking at our friends sitting at their table, watching us with curious eyes.

"Uh, yeah." I ducked my head, searching for what to say. "I'm taking some time off."

"Of course! You should. After your dad..." She trailed off, her voice growing sad. An awkward silence filled the space between us. "So, yeah. Hey, this car is new. It's nice. I always wanted a convertible. Lucky."

"It was my dad's."

MY SOUL TO TAKE

Mandy's face dropped and she rolled her lips, unable to find something else to say. Her eyes shifted to my food and her eyes brightened. "Well, I see you're about to have dinner. I'll just let you go then."

"Yeah, thanks." I put the car back into drive, anxious to be gone.

"I'll see you in class soon?" she asked politely, though her eyes kept darting over her shoulder to our friends. I didn't blame her for wanting to get away from me. Death was never easy to talk about.

"Yeah, sure. I'll see you Monday."

"Great." She waved her hand, backing up. "I'll see you then."

Nodding, I pulled out of the parking lot and turned the car toward the cemetery. I didn't know why I promised to come back on Monday. I wasn't sure if I'd be up to it, but it was the only way I could get her to leave me alone. Now, I could eat my food with my dad in peace.

The gates to the cemetery were locked, but the fence wasn't unclimbable. The drinks would be tricky though. Frowning as I parked, I studied the bars. They weren't big enough for me to squeeze between, but I could put the drinks through the bars and climb over with the rest.

With a plan in place, I climbed out of the car and slowly approached the gate. Placing the drinks on the other side of the bars, I pushed the bag of burgers through as well. It was a tight fit and they'd probably be squished but still edible.

Once that was done, I focused on the gate. I was glad I'd chosen to wear tennis shoes and not my flats. I wasn't the most athletic person, but I thought I could manage it. Thankful for my yoga pants as I shimmied up the gate, I shoved my feet against the sides of the bars as I struggled over the top. My t-shirt caught on the top spikes, scraping my stomach as I fell over the other side with a rip of fabric.

"Fuck," I cursed, the ground knocking the breath out of me. When I got my breathing back under control, I checked my stomach. The scratch wasn't deep, it barely even bled, but my shirt was ruined. Guess I wouldn't be wearing it anymore.

Someone laughed. I spun around, searching for who had done it, but saw no one. Figuring it was my imagination or I was slowly going insane from my lack of exposure to other people, I sighed. Rubbing my grass stained hands on my pants, I gathered my stuff and headed down the walkway.

The cemetery during the day hadn't been so bad, but at night, it was creepy as fuck. Shadows from the trees made my neck twitch as if something might jump out at me at any moment. The tall statues of angels seemed malevolent in the dark. Their praying faces seeming to watch me as I walked past.

Keeping my eyes straight, I searched out the headstone I knew belonged to my dad. When I got to it, I smiled sadly and sat his cup on top of the stone. "Hey, Dad. I'm sorry it took so long for me to come and see you, but look," I held up the bag and grinned. "I brought your favorite." Plopping down on the grass, I pulled out the burger and fries, sitting it on the edge of the stone before grabbing mine.

I unwrapped my burger and took a big bite out of it, enjoying the silence even in the creepy atmosphere. Glancing around as I chewed, I noticed how peaceful it was there. "It's really not as bad as it looks, huh? I guess you could have been put somewhere worse for the afterlife." I stared down at my burger, my throat thickening with emotion. "If there is an afterlife. I don't know. I guess I'm a little lost." I sighed and leaned my arms on my knees, propping them up with my burger hanging between them. "Everyone expects me to get over it and go back to normal. Go back to school. Hang out with my friends. The whole shebang. But I just..." I sniffed and hung my head. "I can't. How do I go on like everything is normal? Like you're not—" my words caught in my throat. "Gone."

"Hey! You there!"

My shoulders bunched up and I jumped to my feet, my eyes darting around. A flashlight shone in my face before I could even think about running. I winced, holding my hand in front of my eyes.

"What are you...oh, it's you!" Edgar, the grounds keeper, shuffled over to me, lowering the flashlight so he wasn't blinding me. "Braxton. It's good to see you. Did you think about my offer?"

I blanked for a moment and then realized he was talking about the job offer. "Uh, honestly, not really. I just wanted to..." My eyes slid over to my dad's headstone and flushed at how crazy I looked, eating at my dad's grave.

However, Edgar didn't seem fazed by it at all. "Of course I understand, but you know, if you worked here, you wouldn't have to sneak into the cemetery." He gestured to the rip in my shirt. "It would certainly save you on your wardrobe at least."

I gave a nervous laugh and pulled at my shirt. "Yeah, I guess that'd be cool." I paused and shot a look around the cemetery once more. It really was nice out here. I could spend the evenings studying. I'd get to hang out with my dad whenever I wanted. Sure, it might be a little creepy, but that was part of its charm. Edgar waited for me with hope in his eyes and I just couldn't say no. "You got yourself a deal." I held my hand out like some kind of idiot, but thankfully Edgar only chuckled and shook it.

"Well then, since you're already out here, why don't we take a tour? Get you settled on what you'll be doing." Edgar adjusted his plaid sweater vest and then gestured with his flashlight to the path.

Following along beside him, I left my food where it was with dad. Nothing but the animals out here would bother it, at least I hoped. "So, what exactly do I have to do?"

"Mostly just walk the grounds, pick up any trash you might see," Edgar explained, one arm behind his back and the other holding the flashlight lighting our way. "We don't get many trespassers." He gave me a sideways look with a hint of mischief in his eyes.

I flushed and ducked my head. "Uh, yeah. Sorry about that. I just couldn't wait."

"Understandable."

We came to a little shack I hadn't noticed before at the funeral. Using a key he pulled out of his pocket, Edgar opened the door and gestured me inside. Really wishing I had my phone because, while I didn't think that Edgar was going to murder me, I still didn't know him and the cemetery thing was putting me on edge.

Scrounging up my courage, I stepped inside and instantly felt better. The small room had a desk to one side with some paperwork spread out in front of a wooden chair. In the middle of the room sat a love seat in front of a small, outdated television. At least I wouldn't be bored out of my mind.

"There's a bathroom over there." Edgar walked into the room, gesturing to a door on the right. "In between your rounds, you can watch television or read. If you have schoolwork, feel free to do it. While the job isn't a hard one. It can be lonely at times."

I nodded, the prospect of working alone not at all a deterrent for me. I walked around the little room taking everything in. Once I made it back to where I'd started, I turned to Edgar. "You mentioned before that the pay was good?"

Edgar smirked, inclining his head. "Ah, yes. Since we work for the city and the position isn't the most desirable, the city will pay you twenty-two an hour plus full benefits. Health and dental."

My mouth gaped. "Whoa, are you sure? That seems a bit excessive." There had to be a catch, there was always a catch.

Chuckling at my shock, Edgar went over to the desk and shuffled some things around. "Here, this would be your schedule and a list of things you would need to do each night."

I took the paper from him, my eyes skimming over it. None of it looked hard. His job continued to seem way too good to be true.

"Do you have any questions?"

I shook my head but then stopped myself, thinking of something. "Yeah, actually, I do." Edgar gestured for me to go ahead. "Why me?"

Edgar took a step toward me with a small smile on his lips. "Because you have something about you, something that needs to be fulfilled,

MY SOUL TO TAKE

and I think this place can help you. Plus," he chuckled, "you were there."

I smiled back at him. The convenience excuse was more believable than the first part. The only thing I was lacking was a giant hole where my dad used to be. Taking a large breath, I pumped my hands at my sides. "When can I start?"

Chapter 3

AUNT CHRISTINE HAD TO go back to work and couldn't hold my hand anymore. Not that I needed hand holding. But it was still nice to have someone there in the empty house.

She lived in St. Louis, all the way up in Missouri. It was nice, but I liked my little town of Hugo, Oklahoma. The summers were blistering, but the winters were mild. I didn't know what I would do if I had to deal with cold weather six months out of the year. Especially not at a new job that required me to walk around outside in the middle of the night.

Thankfully, I only needed a hoodie to keep off the chill tonight. November wasn't quite as warm as October, but it was still balmy enough to keep me from freezing my nipples off.

MY SOUL TO TAKE

Shoving my feet into my tennis shoes, I grabbed my backpack and the keys to Dad's convertible, and headed for the door. I had to admit, I was a bit nervous. Not because it was a new job, but because it was in a cemetery.

Hurrying out the back door, I walked quickly to the car in the evening dusk. I didn't believe in ghosts, goblins, and the like, but nothing good happened after dark. Not unless it's in a bedroom with the creaking springs of a mattress and groans of pleasure.

I sighed as I threw my backpack into the back seat and sat down in front of the steering wheel. I shut the door and cranked the engine. It purred to life like a lounging kitten. I closed my eyes and leaned back against the leather interior, letting the sound soothe my aching heart.

Some hours were good. Others, not so much. This was one of the hours where I wished my dad was still here. I wanted to hear him tell me I'd do a good job. For him to make some crack about keeping my mouth closed in a cemetery.

"Evil spirits will jump inside your body if you mouth off too much near their graves."

Stupid old wives' tale. Some things he did were just silly that way. Even more so was the one where you had to lift your feet when you drove through a yellow light. He still did it though, and I laughed at him.

Fuck.

I rubbed the back of my hand against my wet eyes and sucked in a harsh breath. It came out shaky. My grasp tightened on the steering wheel and then I decided I was done.

Loosening my grip on the wheel, I shifted gears and pulled out of the driveway. I passed the pale blue siding of our house as I drove, followed by the wraparound porch where I had my first kiss, right before my dad flicked on the porch light and embarrassed the shit out of me and my boyfriend.

Derek Miller.

In sixth grade, boyfriends weren't really boyfriends. We said they were, but when you couldn't do anything without your parents driving you it was kind of hard to date. I thought I'd loved him. I knew at the age of thirteen everyone thought they were in love. When he moved away a few months later, it had torn me apart.

But nothing like now.

I supposed blood was stronger than puppy love.

The drive to the cemetery wasn't eventful. Boring, really. I didn't know why it should have been different. It wasn't like I was going to some great destiny. It was just a part-time job.

With great benefits.

I couldn't forget that. I smiled to myself as I pulled up to the cemetery gates. They were open already, even after nightfall. Edgar must have been waiting for me.

I climbed out of the car and grabbed my backpack, pulling the strap over one shoulder. As I walked down the dirt path, I didn't hear a chuckle this time. Only the crickets chirping and the wind blowing through the fallen leaves. The headstones stood silent in their judgment as I moved past them. I was tempted to stop at my dad's grave, but I held back. I didn't trust myself not to break down again. Not with Edgar waiting for me.

The little shack loomed ahead, growing closer with every step I took. I didn't know it then, but this first night would be just the beginning. Nothing would ever be the same after I stepped through that door.

"Ah, Braxton!" Edgar glanced up from the papers on the desk and smiled at me, his eyes crinkling at the sides. "Right on time, I like that. Not many people are punctual nowadays."

I gave him a weak smile in return, shifting my backpack higher on my shoulder. "My dad always said if you're going to be late for anything, make it your death. It's the only time it's acceptable..." My words trailed off as my mind took a dark turn.

Edgar's eyes softened as he pushed away from the desk. "Well, I sure hope I'm late for mine."

I shoved back the darkness and swallowed thickly, nodding. "Me too."

"Alright then. Let's get you settled." Edgar scratched the back of his head and searched around, seeming to forget what he was doing for a second. "Ah!" He lifted a finger and opened a drawer in the desk. Pulling out a set of keys, he handed them over to me. "These are to the gate and the office. Be sure to lock both before you leave in the morning. Friday and Saturday nights are the busiest. You're more likely to have trespassers and partiers. Sundays are quieter. You shouldn't have to worry about anyone showing up then. Most of the kids have class or work the next day."

I inclined my head in understanding. "Okay. Anything else?"

Edgar thought for a moment and then a secretive smile slid up his wrinkled face. "If you see any ghosts, just pretend they aren't there. They'll go away."

"Ghosts?" I startled, my brows rising. "I don't believe in ghosts."

Edgar chuckled. "Then you have nothing to worry about. I left my number on the desk. If you have any questions or find yourself unable to handle the trespassers, give me a call. After you call the police of course. The sirens always scare them off if we don't." His eyes twinkled with mischief.

MY SOUL TO TAKE

I filed the information away for later and rolled the keys over in my hand. "I understand. Have a good night."

"You as well." Edgar patted me on the shoulder as he ambled out of the door. I hadn't seen another car in the parking lot, so I had no idea how Edgar would be getting home, but then again it wasn't my concern. He was an adult and he could take care of himself.

With the place to myself, I sighed and sat my backpack down on the couch in front of the television. Snapping my fingers and then patting my hands on the sides of my thighs, I glanced around the room. It hadn't changed much. There was still a bathroom to the right side and the desk to the left of the door. The couch was rattier than I'd noticed before, an ugly dull blue, and there was a mini fridge and a microwave next to the desk. I guess I didn't have to worry about being hungry at night. I'd packed my lunch today, but now I knew I could bring other kinds of food in the future.

Figuring I should walk the grounds before I got started on my makeup work for class, I grabbed the flashlight off the desk. Making sure my cell was in my hoodie pouch, I shoved the keys into the front pocket of my jeans.

The sun had set, and the stars and moon were out now. I hardly needed the flashlight to see. The path split a few yards from the shack.

Or office, as Edgar had called it. The left led to my dad's grave. I went right.

I'd had my breakdown for the day. I couldn't handle another one tonight.

The path wound through the graves. I took small, slow steps, glancing over the names on the headstones. Erica Norman. Victor Liken. Benjamin Aiks. Peyton Rider.

I stopped.

Staring down at the gravestone, I felt rage billowing in my belly. Before I knew what I was doing, I kicked the stone, wincing as pain radiates through my foot, but I pushed it back. I kicked it again and again, an angry cry ripping from my throat as I beat at my invisible enemy. I knew the stone wasn't him. It wasn't the rich brat who had killed my dad, but it felt damn good to do so.

I collapsed on the ground in front of the grave, my head hanging and tears streaming down my face. I sagged to the ground, dropping the flashlight at my side and letting my fingers dig into the grass beneath me.

After a moment or two, I lifted my head. My eyes scanned the gravestone. Payton Rider. Beloved friend, son, and father. The last one had my brows raising. The dates on his grave put him at twenty-two. Not much older than me. There was a little boy or girl out there who had lost their dad as well.

MY SOUL TO TAKE

It should have quelled my anger, but it only made it worse. Not only had he stolen my dad from me, but he took himself from his own child. My teeth ground together as my fingers curled around the flashlight. I stood and spit on the grave before turning from it.

Before I could walk away in a childish huff, I felt it. Eyes on my back.

"That's a bit harsh, don't you think?" a British, distinctively male voice asked in the dark.

When I spun around, I swung my flashlight up, searching. "Who's there?"

At first, I didn't see him. Then, my flashlight reflected off of something. Pale and almost transparent. A pair of dark brown eyes in a handsome face stared back at me.

A startled cry escaped me as I dropped my flashlight, putting me into shadow. I froze in my fear. I must have fallen asleep in the office. I wasn't crazy. This wasn't real. My eyes were playing tricks on me.

Shoving my trepidation down, I blinked several times and squinted, trying to make out the figure before me.

"What do you have against this person?" The man stepped forward, his form mostly hidden in the dark. "Did he break your heart?"

I scoffed, annoyance replacing my fear. "Fuck no."

"Oh, ho." The man chuckled, shaking his head. "You've got a mouth on you, lady."

Bending down to grab the flashlight, I fumbled with the switch to turn it back on. Pointing in the man's direction, I sucked in a shaky breath. I hadn't been wrong. I could see right through him. He wore his brown hair slightly longer so it brushed his ears. His nose was slightly crooked, like it had been broken and not set right. His lips were prettier than any girl's I'd seen, with a full bottom and thin cupid's bow on top. As if he had a permanent pout on his face.

His clothing was unusual, like he had stepped out of a Shakespearean play. His white, billowy shirt was open at the neck and covered him down to his hands. Brown pants were tucked into soft brown shoes. Either this man had died during a play, or he was...

"You're a ghost?"

Those pouty lips quirked up at one side, one brow arched. "You're a quick one, aren't you? Benedick Cheverell." He bowed at the waist, his arms out to either side. "At your service, my lady."

I snorted. "I'm no lady and you aren't real." With a curl of my lips, I added, "Benedick."

"You can call me Ben, if you so wish, and I'm very much real." He lifted his head and stepped toward me. I flinched back as his fingers skimmed my cheek. His touch was cool and made me shiver before sliding through my skin. "Real enough, in any case."

I lifted the hand with the flashlight and pushed his hand away. To my astonishment, it went straight through him. I shook my head and stepped back. "I don't care who or what you are. You're trespassing."

Ben grinned. "And where do you suppose I go? Hmm? Back to my unholy grave?" His eyes flickered to the right where I assumed his grave sat. "I can't leave the cemetery." He sighed and tucked his thumbs into the front of his pants. "Alas, I am but a prisoner to my resting place. As are the rest of us."

I balked. "The rest of you?" I spun, my flashlight darting around the empty cemetery. "There are more of you?"

Ben chuckled. "Of course. Not everyone gets to go to the great beyond. Some of us," he took a seat on top of Peyton's grave and laced his fingers between his legs, "are left behind."

"Why?" I found myself stepping closer despite myself, lowering the flashlight. Being able to see through him was a bit unsettling.

He shrugged. "Who knows? Only God can answer that question. I'm just here. Until he decides I'm not."

I nodded as if I understood. I didn't. Not a single damn thing. All of this was out of my element. Ghosts. Unfinished business. God. It was just too much for me to handle right now.

"I...I have to go." I moved away from him and turned back the way I came. "I have work to do."

I hurried down the pathway with Ben's voice calling after me.

"I'll see you again, Braxton."

I waved over my shoulder and didn't stop until I was in the office with the door closed tightly behind me. Only then did I relax, and then I asked myself, "How did he know my name?"

Chapter 4

AFTER I GOT MY heart to stop pounding in my chest, I set about pretending what had happened, hadn't happened. Just like Edgar said, if I ignore him, he'll go away...right?

It wasn't the healthiest solution, but it was the one I had.

Moving across the room, I grabbed my backpack off the couch and went about getting my make-up work out. I spread the books and papers across the desk on the other side of the office and plopped down in my chair. Pulling my phone out, I turned a premade playlist I liked to work by and focused on the work in front of me and not the handsome ghost outside the office door.

My plan worked.... for about an hour. Then, while I was pouring over my calculus work, a voice asked by my ear, "What in the nine hells is this torture?"

A scream ripped from my throat, and I jumped in my seat, spinning around to see the Shakespearean ghost staring at my homework with the most perplexed expression. For some reason, call it a result of just losing my dad or maybe even insanity, I wasn't scared by his presence. I was...annoyed. Yeah, that's the word I was looking for.

Narrowing my eyes on him, I spun back around in the desk chair and faced my work once more. "It's called calculus."

"I do not care what you lot call them. It looks like something Lucifer himself would bring out for the most heinous crimes." His British accent made every word sound far more intriguing than it actually was and made it near impossible to ignore him.

"Alright, Shakespeare," I shifted in my seat to glare at the ghost.

"Ben," he corrected me. He leaned against the edge of the desk with a smirk on his lips, and his arms crossed over his muscular chest.

I frowned and waved a hand in between us. "Whatever. How are you doing that?"

"Doing what?" Shakespeare frowned and dropped his arms.

"Leaning against the desk when you couldn't touch me earlier." My brows furrowed as I tried to figure him out. "And what about the tombstone? You sat on that too."

Shakespeare shrugged. "Alas, I do not know. I simply am. What can one do but accept their existence for what it is when they are dead?" He gave me a forlorn smile, reminding me that I was talking to a dead person.

I sat my pencil down on the desk with a snap and spun my chair around. "Alright, not that I'm accepting this whole ghost thing, because I'm still not sure I'm not dreaming." Muttering under my breath, I added, "Or having a nervous breakdown."

What did it matter? If he was a ghost or not? He couldn't touch me. All he could do was annoy me to death. And that at least kept the night from being boring. I had a feeling this job could have its down points—a lot of them.

"I can assure you, lovely lady," Shakespeare turned a smoldering look in my direction, leaning in close. "I am quite real. I'd be happy to show you?" He grabbed hold of his shirt and began unbuttoning the buttons.

Snapping my eyes closed, I held my hands up in front of me as if to ward off his nakedness. "Nope. I'm good. Thanks anyway."

Shakespeare chuckled in what sounded like a safe distance away from me that I opened my eyes once more. His buttons were all done back up the way they were, and his hands were tucked into his pockets.

I frowned. "You are so confusing."

"How so?"

Pushing up off the chair, I moved closer to him, inspecting every aspect of him closely. "You're nothing like I imagined a ghost would be." If you ignored the slight transparency, he could be just another person. One who liked to cosplay, but still any other average Joe on the street. "Why aren't you trying to hurt me?"

Shakespeare cocked his head to one side. "Why on God's green earth would I want to hurt such a gorgeous creature such as yourself?"

I shrugged. "I don't know. Based on all the movies I've ever seen, ghosts are supposed to be malevolent spirits who are jealous of the living, so they want to bring them to the other side."

His lips curled up in amusement. "The only jealousy I have is for the sun that gets to caress your lovely face."

I snorted.

"What have I said?"

Waving a hand in his direction, I laughed, "You're living up to your look, is all."

"My...look," he drew out slowly. "Whatever do you mean?"

I moved closer to him, gesturing at his clothing. "Oh, you know the whole Shakespeare thing you have going on here. Your clothes. The way you speak. It's all very...cliché."

MY SOUL TO TAKE

Now it was his turn to laugh. "Shakespeare? You mean that self-important drunkard? Spouting off his nonsense to anyone who would hear it? I am appalled you would think so lowly of me on our first meeting."

I gaped at him. "You knew Shakespeare?" This ghost just became ten times more interesting than my calculus. Okay, that wasn't much of a stretch. Everything was more interesting than calculus.

He shrugged his shoulder. "I knew of him before I sailed to the New World and found my end at the hands of the natives." He let out a bitter laugh. "Who would have known that we would be the intruders to a supposedly undiscovered land."

Nodding in understanding, I had the urge to pat him on the shoulder but thought better of it. I wasn't sure I could handle my hand going through him just yet. "Understandable. The history books are still playing catch up to the actual events." I snorted and laughed. "If only they had a ghost to give them a firsthand account."

Ben smiled at me. "That would be something."

"Well, as much as I want to stand here and keep talking to you," I paused as Ben beamed at me, causing my face to heat. "I do have work to do."

A loud crash outside made my body jerk.

"And it seems like I have my work cut out for me." Sighing, I grabbed my flashlight and the keys to the office and bolted out the door.

Ben trailed behind me like a cold wind on my back. Did ghosts walk? Or did they float? I didn't have the time to find out for sure. I was hired for a job, and that was what I was going to do.

My tennis shoes crunched the leaves on the ground as I hurried toward the ruckus. Now that I was outside and headed in that direction, I could hear voices and drunken laughter. A spurt of light appeared a few yards away, lighting up the cemetery.

"They did not seriously make a fire in the middle of the cemetery?" I asked myself, forgetting for a moment that I wasn't alone.

"It does seem that way," Ben commented beside me, making me jump once more.

"Geez, make some sound, would you?" I snapped at him before turning back to my trespassers. "Do they all have this lack of respect for the dead?"

Ben shrugged. "We're dead. What do we care?"

I pursed my lips. "That doesn't matter. You deserve as much respect as the living, and they have no right to be desecrating someone's loved one's grave." Thinking about how I'd feel if someone treated my dad's that way, a righteous fury settled in my chest as I made my way to the burning light in the middle of the dark.

MY SOUL TO TAKE

When I was in hearing distance, I pointed my flashlight and said in my most authoritative voice, "Hey, you're not supposed to be here." A small group of frat guys, each with a girl hanging off their arms, all turned toward the sound of my voice.

"Shit! Old man Edgar!" one of the frat guys who had been working on a keg tossed the hose down and bolted across the cemetery.

"Chase, chill.," one of the other guys called out. "It's just some chick." With no respect for the woman currently clinging to him, the guy gave me a flirtation look. "Hey, why don't you come have a drink with us?"

Frowning, I stepped further into their little party. "No, I won't have a drink with you, and if you don't leave, I'm calling the cops. This is a cemetery, a place for mourning and remembrance, not so you can start an illegal fire and give these girls, who could really do better, a five-second thrill."

"Hey, you can't talk to us like that." Another frat guy snapped, pulling away from his date to meet me in the middle. "I think it's time for you to leave."

Standing my ground, I met his glare for one of my own. "Actually, I can. I work here. And I say you're gone. Unless you'd like a call to..." I glanced at the Greek letters next to the college logo embroidered onto his polo shirt. Richmond

College, of course. "...the dean of Richmond about their precious fraternity."

The guy scoffed. "Like he would listen to you. You're nobody. Probably go to the local college."

"Actually, I do." I crossed my arms over my chest and smirked. "And I actually happen to know Dean Withers personally." I pulled my phone out. "Maybe we should call him now? Do you think that he'd still be up this hour?"

The guy who had tried to hit on me placed his hand on the other guy's shoulder. "Come on, man. It's not worth it. Let's go."

For a moment, I thought the guy wasn't going to listen to his friend, but then he gave me a final glare before turning a dazzling smile to his date. "Come on, babe. Let's get out of here."

The others followed suit except for one, who came back for the keg. He didn't seem as pissed as the others. Just sad. "So you know, we were here to mourn a friend."

I crossed my arms and arched a brow. "Oh yeah? Well, I hope wherever they are, they didn't see this lack of respect you've shown here."

He shrugged, lifting the keg onto his beefy shoulders. "I don't know. Rider would have liked it, I think. But what do I know, I was only his roommate for the last three years."

"Rider?" My arms dropped, and scowled. "Peyton Rider?"

"You knew him?"

My jaw tightened as I bit out, "Yeah. My dad was the one in the other car."

His eyes widened, and then after a moment, the guy nodded his head. "I get it. We both lost someone dear to us that day. I'm sorry for your loss. But try to remember other people are suffering too." He shifted the keg upon his shoulder. "Your pain isn't the only one that matters."

My hand tightened on the flashlight until the sides of it bit into my hand. "I know that."

"Then maybe show it." He walked away before I could say anything more.

Muttering to myself about idiot frat guys not knowing what they were talking about, I dumped some dirt onto the fire until it was down to embers.

"My, you have quite a bit of fire in you. Really gave those lurkers the what for." Ben appeared into the clearing, kicking a bit of dirt toward the ash and wood.

"Yeah, and you were no help whatsoever, Dick." I scowled, turning my back on him and moving back toward the path. I stopped briefly at the grave they had been partying on.

Peyton Fucking Rider. Even in death, I couldn't get rid of the reminder of how my dad was stolen from me. For a moment, I remembered what the frat guy had said. My pain wasn't the only one that mattered? Of course, I knew that. I wasn't a complete bitch. I was entitled to my own pain just as much as they were, wasn't I?

"You really despise that man," Ben stared down at the grave with a curious frown. "What did he do to you?"

I sighed and wrapped my arms around myself as I sludged down the path. "He killed my dad."

Chapter 5

AS I STALKED BACK to the office, Shakespeare disappeared to wherever ghosts vanished to. Relieved to be alone, I slammed the door to the office, wincing as the shack shook slightly. For all its pleasant interior, it was still just a wooden shack.

I threw the flashlight down on the desk and flopped down on the couch face first. Burying my face in a throw pillow, I screamed.

I screamed until my throat went raw, and the urge to cry subsided. I screamed until I no longer saw the frat guy's stupid hurt face. Until my mind and heart went numb from all the heartache.

My arm swiped over my face as I pushed myself up into a sitting position. I sniffled and stared at the black screen of the television. This had been a bad idea. Who was I to think I could handle working here?

Sure, I could see my dad every day. There was also the reminder of the person who took him away from me. If it wasn't the grave of Peyton Rider, then it was those who were here to mourn him too. I didn't know if I could handle it.

Sucking a sharp breath in, I forced myself off the couch. I'd finish the night out and then tell Edgar I was quitting. He'd just have to find someone else to watch the cemetery.

Happy with my decision, I went back to the desk where my calculus still sat. My nose scrunched up in dismay. I wasn't really in the mood for homework anymore, but it had to be done. Just then, my stomach rumbled, reminding me I hadn't eaten since earlier that evening.

With an alternative plan, I pulled my lunch out of the bag and slowly worked away at my ham sandwich—anything to make the time go faster. When I was finished eating and cleaned up my mess, I glanced at the clock on my phone and groaned.

"Fuck." I laid my head down on the desk. It was barely midnight. I still practically had the whole night ahead of me. I didn't know how I would get through tonight, let alone any future nights. Yep. It was the right decision to quit.

MY SOUL TO TAKE

Looking at my homework again, I shook my head and grabbed my flashlight and phone instead.

"Better make the rounds again," I said to the empty office.

This time as I walked down the eerie path, there were no partiers, no one trying to sneak in a midnight voodoo session or even one annoying British ghost. There was only me, the graves, and the creepy as hell stone statues.

Why did they put statues of angels up in cemeteries anyway? It wasn't like they were going to guard the dead or anything. The headstones I got. You needed to know where each body was buried for the family, and well, you couldn't very well bury one body on top of the other. Though, when I thought about it, if we buried people vertically rather than horizontally, we'd save so much more room in the cemetery. Though, I guess the whole laid to rest thing would be obsolete.

I chuckled to myself.

"You should laugh more," a voice from the left said. The voice was a pleasant baritone, but it didn't make me scream any less to hear it.

"Who's there?" I called out, shining my flashlight in the direction of the trespasser.

"Nobody of importance," the voice replied as I shone the light by a tree. The silhouette of a guy just barely visible appeared.

Stepping closer to the tree, I squinted in the dark. "You're not supposed to be out here."

"Nowhere else to go." The guy's shoulders shrugged. Shoulders that I could now make out as transparent and covered in a letterman's jacket.

I scoffed. "Geez, how many ghosts live here?" I paused and frowned. "I mean, not that you live here, but you know, exist?" I rambled on, trying to figure out a way not to offend him.

The guy chuckled.

Stopping my rambles, I glared at him. "Just go haunt someone else, why don't you? I have work to do."

Shifting in place, the guy shrugged again. "Fine." I spun away from him, and then he said, "Go back to staring at your calculus book. Question number five is wrong, by the way. You added rather than subtracted your cosine."

Turning back to the ghost, I snapped, "How do you know...that?" He was already gone.

Frowning even harder, I walked the rest of the cemetery in deep thought, my eyes searching for the new ghost every once in a while. Who was he? How did he know about my homework? There's no way I was wrong. Calculus was something I was actually good at. Except when I arrived back at the office and checked my work page, sure enough, he was right.

I searched the office for any sign of the ghost but found nothing. Were they able to see me without being present? Apparently so, otherwise, the whole cemetery would be filled with spirits all the time.

The why and how I could even see ghosts hadn't even crossed my mind. If they could appear to anyone or if it was just me? If so, why didn't they appear to their family members who came to visit? Surely, someone would have mentioned it before now. The likelihood of this all being just in my head was becoming more and more likely.

The rest of the evening was, thankfully, ghost-free. Then at the wee hours of the morning, when the sun finally began to peek over the horizon, Edgar came through the office door. He glanced around the room, and a crooked smile landed on me.

"Ah, you survived."

I arched a brow as I stood and yawned. "Were you worried?"

Shaking his head, Edgar shuffled into the room. "No, not at all. So, how was it?"

Gathering my things, I opened my mouth to tell him what I'd decided but stopped. Instead of quitting, what came out of my mouth surprised even me. "It was great. Besides scaring off some frat guys earlier in the evening."

Edgar frowned. "I hope they didn't give you too much trouble."

"Nope," I shook my head and smiled. "No trouble at all. See you later."

His worn hand stopped me. "You're coming back tonight?"

I cocked my head to the side. "Of course. It's on the schedule." Leaving him with a confused expression, I made my way to my dad's convertible. Or rather mine. I had to remember that.

As I drove home, I tried to puzzle together why I had changed my mind. I hadn't consciously done it. Up until Edgar had walked through the door, I had every intention of quitting, and still, I didn't. Why?

Too tired to dwell on it, I focused on getting home. When I arrived, I didn't even bother changing my clothes. I kicked my shoes off and climbed into bed. My eyes were shut before I even hit the pillow.

Aunt Christine was waiting for me in the kitchen when I came down a good seven hours later.

"Hey, sleepyhead. I was wondering when you'd wake up." She handed me a cup of coffee with a grin.

"Thanks." I cupped it in my hands and took a long sip of the hot liquid.

"How's the new job coming?" She asked, leaning against the kitchen counter.

I shrugged. "It's alright. Pretty boring, really." I stared at her for a moment. "Aren't you supposed to be back in St. Louis?"

MY SOUL TO TAKE

Aunt Christine shrugged. "I had a feeling I should check on you, so I left early after work yesterday and arrived pretty late. I'm surprised you didn't see my car in the driveway."

I glanced out the window and shrugged a shoulder. "I was too tired, I guess."

"You better make sure your sleep schedule aligns with school, or you'll be snoozing away that college tuition." She wagged a motherly finger at me.

Nodding, I sat my cup down on the island. "I'll work on that. I have classes in the morning on Monday, so I'll be sure to make myself stay up."

"You're going back?" Her brows shot to her hairline.

I turned from her quizzical look and opened the fridge. "Yeah, I thought it was time. Plus, if I miss too much more, I'll have to take an incomplete and redo the classes. I can't afford that." I grabbed the eggs and butter out of the fridge and shut the door. "Eggs?"

"No, thanks." Aunt Christine waved me off. "I already ate."

"I don't know why, but I'm starving. I feel like I could eat a horse." I told her as I worked through three, four, six eggs. Adding some salt and pepper and a dash of garlic, I scrambled them together with a whisk.

"That's night shift for you. Throws your whole clock out of whack." Aunt Christine explained as

I began to cook my eggs. "Have you seen any ghosts yet?"

I jerked, and my arm went into the hot pan. "Ouch, fuck!"

"Braxton," Aunt Christine cried out, rushing over to me. She turned the burners off and pushed the pan aside before taking my hand in hers. "Let me see." She pulled me over to the sink and turned on the water. "It's not too bad. Just a bit red," my aunt reassured me as she put my arm under the cool water. "Now, you're going to want to put something on this, or it will blister."

"I know, Aunt Christine," I groaned as the water made the burn ache a little less. "It's not my first burn, you know."

Aunt Christine gave me a mothering look before sighing. "You're right. You're an adult. You can take care of yourself." She stepped away from the sink and wiped her hands off on a hand towel. "I guess I should take this sea salt chocolate to the neighbor kids. Maybe they need some he-"

"No," I grabbed her by the waist and hugged her. "Did I say I didn't need your help? I don't remember saying such a thing. What are you talking about?" I hugged her to me tightly as she laughed and patted my hands.

"That's what I thought."

After I wrapped up my burn, I was put off the eggs. Instead, I ate another ham sandwich. I was going to have to buy some more at this rate.

MY SOUL TO TAKE

"So, what had you so freaked?" Aunt Christine asked, sitting next to me on the couch. "Was it something I said? Cause you know I was just joking about the ghosts, right?" She placed her hand on my arm with concern on her face.

I gave a noncommittal shrug and chewed on my sandwich. "It was nothing. A muscle spasm."

She arched a brow at me. "Must have been some spasm."

"Yeah," I chuckled nervously. Licking my lips, I turned to her cautiously. "Uh, hey, speaking of ghosts. Have you ever seen one?"

Aunt Christine's brows lifted. At first, I thought she was just going to laugh at me and reassure me that there was no such thing, but then she stopped and thought about it. "You know, I don't tell many people this because well, I'm not sure if I even believe it myself, but when I was a little girl," she began, her voice going low so that I had to lean in to hear her. "When my grandma died, I swore I saw her ghost at the wake."

My brows furrowed. "At the wake? Not at the cemetery?"

"No, it was here in this very house," she glanced around the living room. "Grandpa bought this house for them when they were first married. Then it passed to my dad after they both died, then your dad, and now you. I always wondered if she still lingered around to keep an eye on us." She giggled to herself and then sighed. "It's silly, I know. But it's nice to think about."

"Yeah," I murmured, staring off at the wall. "It's a nice thought."

Aunt Christine had given me something to think about. If she had seen my great grandma's ghost lingering here, then what Shakespeare had told me wasn't right. The ghosts could leave the cemetery. Or at least some of them could. I wondered what kept certain ghosts there and others away. Did it have to do with how they were buried?

"Aunt Christine?" I called out to her as she stood to leave the room.

She turned to me. "Hmm?"

"Where was she buried?"

She gave me a perplexing frown. "Who?"

"Great-grandma."

"Oh, she wasn't. Buried that is." She smiled sadly. "Grandma always wanted to be cremated. She didn't like the idea of her body rotting in the ground, even if her priest had a field day about it."

"So, where are her remains at then?"

Aunt Christine tapped her chin and thought. "You know, I'm not sure. They stayed in a pretty pink and white urn until the end of the wake, and then your great-grandpa did something with them." She shrugged. "I would say to ask your dad, but..."

"Yeah," I trailed off. "I can't. Thanks anyway."

Chapter 6

AS I PACKED MY lunch for work, a part of me was excited and yet terrified of seeing the ghosts again. Would I see Shakespeare again or maybe the letterman jacket guy? The idea of seeing either of them again was a bit thrilling. The prospect that it was all in my head, and I was going crazy was not.

"How long are you staying for?" I asked Aunt Christine as I pulled on my tennis shoes and grabbed my coat.

"I need to head back tomorrow. It's over an eight-hour drive. And this gal needs her beauty sleep." She grinned at me before shoveling a forkful of Lo Mein into her mouth. "Sure you don't want to take some for work?"

I shook my head and smiled. "No, thanks. Chinese never tastes the same the second time around."

"You're crazy," Aunt Christine said with her mouth full.

I waved her off and laughed. I loved my Aunt Christine. She was just this side of mothering and the fun big sister type—best of both worlds. I didn't know what I would do if I didn't have her here during this time.

Swallowing a lump in my throat as emotion attempted to take me over, I left the house before she could see me. The last thing I needed was for her to think I was falling apart all over again.

You've got this, Braxton. You're a strong independent woman who doesn't believe in ghosts. Don't let one night of weirdness send you spiraling into the loony bin of sadness and despair.

My mind zoned out as I drove to work. I didn't even remember stopping at any red lights or the drive there. I was just suddenly at the gates of the cemetery, and it all became real again. As panic began to well up in my chest, Edgar appeared, stopping it.

"Braxton, so good to see you. Are you ready for another fun-filled evening?" his eyes crinkled at the edges as he smiled at me.

I smiled despite myself. "Yep. Ready and willing." I climbed out of my dad's convertible and pulled my bag over my shoulder. I met up with Edgar at the gate. "Anything else I need to know?"

Edgar's face went serious for a moment. "Now that you mention it, I did forget to tell you last night to stay away from the creek that runs along the back of the cemetery."

My smile wilted. "Why? Is it haunted or something?" I said it jokingly, but inside I was shaking. If he was warning me off somewhere, then it had to be worse than what I had seen so far, right?

Shaking his head and hand at me, Edgar chuckled. "No, no. A lot of animals are attracted to the area, and I wouldn't want to lose you to a coyote or something."

"Oh," I sighed, my shoulders sagging. "I mean, good. And I won't. Go near it, I mean."

"Good. Then I will be off." Edgar patted me on the arm as he walked past me. "Have a good evening, Braxton."

"You too." I waved after him, frowning. Was he going to walk home? There wasn't a car in the drive. I shrugged. Whatever. It wasn't my decision to make for him. Perhaps he lived close by.

Pushing the thoughts of Edgar walking home aside, I made my way to the office. The sun had just gone over the horizon, and the cemetery had fallen into shadow. My eyes skittered around the walkway, searching for either of my ghostly visitors.

"So far, so good," I muttered to myself as I entered the office and tossed my bag down.

"You really shouldn't let the old man walk alone, you know."

I jumped and spun around, my fist raised. When I saw Shakespeare leaning against the nearby wall, eating an apple, I huffed. "Geez Louis, don't fucking do that!"

"Mouthy little thing, you are," he commented, biting into the shiny red apple.

Pursing my lips, I stared at him. "You haven't seen mouthy yet. And how are you doing that? You're dead," I waved a hand up and down his transparent form. "You don't need to eat."

Shakespeare eyed the apple and shrugged. "I could not tell you. I just thought I'd love an apple right now, and it appeared." He licked his lips where the impossible juices laid. "Sad, though."

"What?"

"I can't taste a damn bit." He tossed the apple, and it disappeared, just like that. No poof. It was just gone.

"This is so weird." I sighed and sank down on the edge of the couch.

He pushed away from the wall and stood before me. "It is no more strange to you than it is to me. And I'm dead."

"So, you haven't talked to a living person before? It's just me?" I cocked my head to the side, unable to believe it's true. If it was, then what did that say about me? Was I the weirdo? Was there something wrong with me?

Shakespeare shrugged. "I've talked to plenty of the living, just none of them have ever graced me with speaking back. Not until you."

"I don't know if I should feel special or freaked out." I hugged my arms around my torso, staring down at the ground.

He knelt before me, his misty dark eyes staring into mine. "You should feel whatever it is your heart tells you. Trying to force yourself to feel something you do not, will not answer your questions any more than I could."

A little annoyed by his whimsical explanation, I huffed, "Don't you ever talk like a normal person?"

Arching a brow, Shakespeare gave me a bemused smile. "Whatever do you mean?"

"Never mind." I shook my head and leaned against the back of the couch. Giving the ghost before me a long look, I asked, "So how'd you kick the bucket?"

"I do not know this phrase?" Shakespeare stood and stared down at me with a frown. "Why would I need to kick a bucket?"

Throwing my head back, I laughed at him. While I laughed at the confused British ghost, I leaned a little too far back and fell backward with a, 'Whoops!' which only made me laugh harder. I collapsed onto the couch and then bounced onto the floor. I hit it with a loud thud and a groan.

Shakespeare appeared at my side.

"Are you quite well? Do you need a doctor?" The grave concern on his expression only served to start me on another laughing fit. "I do not see what is so humorous. I do believe you might have an injury in your head. Perhaps even bleeding." He continued, examining me with his dark eyes. No doubt finding no external injury, he murmured to himself, "Or maybe madness runs in your family."

Finally getting a hold of myself, I pushed myself into a seated position. "No, I'm not injured. Though, I wouldn't rule out the madness. I am beginning to believe there has to be some kind of crazy in there for me even to comprehend the fact that I'm talking to a dead guy like it's just another Saturday night."

"It is for me." Shakespeare shrugged.

"Fine. You win. You're dead. You're here. I'll get over it. Eventually." I smiled at him, the reference obviously lost on the man several centuries outside his time. "What I meant was, how did you die?"

"Oh," Shakespeare sat on the coffee table that I had barely missed on my way down, putting me right at his crotch level.

My face burning furiously, I climbed up on the couch, keeping my eyes down.

"As I said before, the natives were not happy we had taken their land and..." he sighed, shaking his head. "It is not something that one should discuss with someone with a delicate constitution such as yourself."

My mouth dropped open in a gape as I stared at him. "Excuse the fuck out of me. Who has a delicate constitution?"

Shakespeare gestured in my direction. "Why women, of course. You are soft creatures meant to be protected from the horrors of the world. I will not sully your precious ears with the tale of my demise."

"You're lucky you're already dead because I'm about to be the reason for your demise, right now." I raised a tightly curled fist in his direction.

He frowned, confused. "I do not understand. Have I offended you in some way?"

Realizing his confusion was genuine, I sighed heavily, reluctantly dropping my fists to my lap. "For someone who has been haunting this place for several centuries, you sure don't keep up with the times."

Shakespeare shrugged. "I am afraid you are right. We cannot interact the way we wish we could, and those I see are here for mourning, not socializing. I do not know what has become of the world outside the looming gates of my prison. Though," he paused in thought. "I am not sure I want to."

I huffed and crossed my arms over my chest. "Well, if you want to keep interacting with me, you need to know that women," I emphasized, "are just as capable as men, if not more so. We have careers, lives, and even minds of our own. Men are the ones who are becoming obsolete." I pointed out quite proudly as I watched his expression sink. "I can have a baby all on my own. No male involvement required."

He stared at me in one-part horror and the other part awe. "How is this even fathom some? Do you not need the man's seed?"

I couldn't help the grin that spread over my face. "Nope. Not anymore. There's a whole thing about taking stem cells to create a baby without needing a sperm donor at all."

"Stem cells? Sperm donor?" Shakespeare's head looked like it was ready to explode. "There must be witchcraft now for such a thing to have happened."

"Nope," I popped the word. "It's science. And I for one-" my words were cut off as a man in a leather jacket came barreling through the office door.

"Yo, Brit. There's some trouble down by the creek. You need to be attending to." Mr. Leather's pale blue eyes landed on me, and the unlit cigarette hanging from his mouth perked up. "Now, who is this sweet piece of cherry pie?"

"This," Shakespeare stood and gestured toward me. "This is Braxton, our new weekend caretaker." Mr. Leather opened his mouth to say something, but Shakespeare cut him off. "And you will treat her with the respect a lady of her quality deserves." He gave Mr. Leather a firm look

MY SOUL TO TAKE

before turning to me. "Please excuse me. There is something I must attend to." With those words, he disappeared.

"Alone at last," Mr. Leather strutted over to me, sliding both hands over the sides of his slicked-back hair so black and full of product that the light gleamed off it. How that was even possible for someone who was transparent and well dead, I didn't know. I was beginning to wonder why I even bothered to question any of it anymore.

"I need to make my rounds," I quickly explained as he prowled toward me.

"That's alright. I'll come with you." He shoved his hands in the pockets of his tight-fitting jeans, the bottoms rolled up above his combat boots. "It ain't exactly kosher for a gal of your caliber to be wandering these grounds alone, you dig?"

I arched a brow. "No, I don't. I've been doing alright on my own so far. So, thanks but no thanks."

Apparently, Mr. Leather couldn't take a hint, even a blatant one, and continued to follow me out of the office. We walked down the path for a few moments with Mr. Leather trailing behind me. I could practically feel his eyes on my ass the whole way and was just about sick of it.

"So," he sucked his teeth around his cigarette. "What's a delectable piece like you doing working in a God-forsaken place like this?"

I spun around and pointed my flashlight at him. "If you don't stop talking about me like I'm some sort of floozy you probably gallivanted around with when you were alive, I'm going to make sure you spend the rest of eternity listening to nothing but smooth jazz." I took a gamble that his type wouldn't be caught dead listening to anything so classy and was right on the mark when Mr. Leather winced.

"Ouch. Right in the kisser." He jerked his leather jacket with both hands and shifted his shoulders. "Look, we got off on the wrong foot," he held his hand out to me, "I'm Rooster."

I stared at his hand for a long moment before placing my hand on top of his. Coolness met my skin, and for a brief moment, the pressure of his hand was there, and then it was gone. Not letting myself dwell on it, I shook my head. "Fine. Rooster, is it? Just stay out of my way and keep your comments to yourself."

"Whatever you say, boss." His lips quirked up as he readjusted his cigarette.

I huffed and turned away from him. "And don't call me boss."

Chapter 7

"SO, HOT MAMA, WHAT'S on the menu tonight?" Rooster moved up beside me along the path. "We gonna hang? Or maybe call the Fuzz on some candy asses?"

Looking at him from the corner of my eye, I sighed and tried to ignore him.

"Or we can get in your flip top and do the backseat bingo," Rooster's breath hit my neck in a chilly breeze, making me shiver.

I jerked to a stop and pivoted around. Pointing a finger into his transparent body, which was way weirder than I expected, I snapped, "I don't understand half of the words that are coming out of your mouth, but I can take a good guess." I stepped up close and glared up into Rooster's face. "I'm not your boss, I'm not your hot mama. And no, I don't want to play backseat bingo. So, either be quiet or go away." I gave him one more poke, not that I knew how much good it did since it kept going through his body.

"Come on, sugar, don't flip your lid. I'm just teasing." Rooster kept following after me, not at all deterred by my words.

I let out a loud groan and threw my hands up in the air. "What do I have to do to do my job in peace?"

Rooster grinned and wagged his brows. "I could think of a few choice activities." He pulled his lower lip between his teeth and looked me over with a heated gaze.

Rolling my eyes, I shook my head. "Not gonna happen." I wanted to ask if it was even possible, but bringing the subject back up for discussion didn't seem like a good idea.

"What do you say, dolly?" He trailed a cold finger down the side of my face.

I moved away from his hand, walking straight through him without answering his question. I kept walking forward, hoping that the ghost had taken the hint when Rooster appeared next to me. Determined not to let him bother me, I tried a different strategy.

"So, Rooster," I huffed a laugh. "That can't be your real name? No parents are that cruel."

Rooster didn't answer, and for a moment, I thought he had left me. A turn of my head told me that he was still there. His face no longer joking. His lips curled down into a tight frown, and his eyes cast down on the ground before him. His incorporeal boots kicked the ground and little tuffs of dirt puffed into the air.

"What, no answer?" I teased, grinning at him. "I thought you wanted to hang. And now you won't even talk to me?"

He snorted and dragged a hand through his hair. "Francis. Francis Adams."

I was quiet for a long moment before chuckling. "Now I know why you go by Rooster. With a name like Francis, you were bound to get beat up as a kid."

Glancing at him out of the corner of my eye, I was happy to see that smirk back on his face. "No way, doll face. No one gets the jump on Rooster."

"Oh yeah? You were a badass, huh?" I scanned the cemetery, my flashlight hitting the top of each headstone as we passed them.

"Damn straight." He slicked back his hair and shoved another unlit cigarette between his teeth. Must be a habit from when he was alive.

We walked in silence for a few moments before I broke it. "Money. I work here for the money. And well," I paused as we came back around to where my dad's grave sat, "for my dad."

Rooster squatted down to read the headstone before glancing back at me. "Sorry, Braxton. I didn't know about your pops. That must be a major bummer."

I shrugged. "Not as bad as being a ghost stuck in a cemetery."

"Oh, right where it hurts." Rooster grabbed his chest, and fake died on the ground. I laughed and tried to nudge him with my foot, but it went through him. When he didn't immediately get back up, I knelt beside him. "Come on, it's not funny anymore. Get up."

When he still didn't get up, I leaned over him and searched for how to touch him. Did I check his pulse? Wait, that was stupid. He's a ghost. They don't have pulses. Could a ghost even die? What the hell was I supposed to do?

"I don't know what to do. Wake up, Rooster," I shouted into his face, my eyes wide and my heart racing in my chest. "This isn't cool. Or jazzy. Whatever the fucking slang you use."

"Jesus H. Christ, you've got a mouth on you," Rooster's eyes popped open as he grinned.

I gasped in relief and then growled, swatting at his transparent body. "That wasn't funny, Rooster. I thought you really died."

Rooster sat up on his elbows and grinned. "Babe, I'm already dead. I can't get much deader." He pulled on his face with one hand. When I didn't laugh, he frowned. "Were you really that worried about me? Little ol' Rooster?"

I crossed my arms and turned my face away from him. "I wasn't worried. Like you said, you're already dead. I just didn't want you to go poof on my watch."

That chilly breath touched my ear. "I've got somethin' else that you could make go poof instead."

Scowling, I twisted around to shove him away. Instead, I fell straight through him and right into a nearby tombstone. A sharp sting lanced through my forehead. Gasping in pain, I rolled over to my back and touched my forehead. Blood, dark in the night light, came away from the wound.

"Great. Just great." I grumbled and pushed up on my hands and knees. My world spun, and I sat back down.

"Are you alright, Braxton?" Rooster knelt beside me. His hand went to my forehead. "Yowch. That looks like it bites."

"No kidding," I shouted at him and winced. "Just give me a minute. The world has to stop spinning."

Rooster pressed his lips together into a thin line as he stared down at me. "I could try and carry you back? But," he paused and scratched the back of his head. "I'm not the best at going full corporeal. Want me to get the Brit?"

I shook my head, and that made it worse. "No," I gasped. "I'll be fine. Just stop talking and... stop moving around. Wait. Are there two of you now?"

"Fuck." Rooster cursed before it all went black.

Chapter 8

I CAME TO SLOWLY. My head ached something fierce, and the thought of even opening my eyes made me want to vomit.

"Is she going to bite it?" Rooster's voice came from somewhere.

My ears seemed to be working fine, at least.

"No, she's not going to die," another voice I didn't quite recognize snapped at Rooster.

I tried my best to stay still. The soft but springy object underneath me was familiar enough. I had to be on the couch in the office. That was good news—nothing like bleeding out on someone's grave.

While I might be going crazy with all the ghost interactions, the pain in my head was real enough. I tried to focus on the voices around me and not the throbbing in my head.

"I'm tellin' ya, she needs a doctor."

I agreed there. A nice doctor with a morphine tap? Sounded like heaven to me.

"And how exactly do you plan on getting here there, genius?" asked the voice that was beginning to sound clearer every second. I laid there and listened, he sounded annoyed but a bit panicked.

"Well, you've got me there, College Boy." Rooster huffed. Cold air touched my ankle, and I flinched. "Yo, College Boy, I think she's waking up." The cold air moved closer to me, and I shifted away from it, making my head ache even more. "Hey, doll face. You awake in there?"

I groaned, a hand coming up to my head. Something crusty and partially wet came away on my hand. Unable to keep them closed any longer, I squinted into the pale light of the office. First, going to Rooster kneeling beside me, a concerned expression on his transparent face, then to my hand. Dark brownish red-stained it, making me groan again. Why is it that every time you see blood, it hurts ten times worse?

"What happened?" I asked, clearing my throat against the dryness.

"You fell into a headstone." Rooster told me with a chuckling huff. "You really shouldn't try to tattle a ghost; you're going to mess up that sweet, sweet bod of yours."

MY SOUL TO TAKE

I gave him the side-eye as I tried to sit up. Each movement felt like I was moving through sticky taffy.

"Give her some room, man," the other voice in the room commanded Rooster, who had gotten even closer to me, sending a chill down my spine.

My head whipped toward the sound, and I instantly regretted it. Clutching my head with both hands, I squinted out at the speaker. The letterman's jacket was the first thing I noticed, then the shaggy sandy hair falling over a pair of sad blue eyes. My mystery ghost from yesterday. Great.

"I'm just trying to make sure she's alright, Champ. No need to be a tightwad." Rooster shifted away from me, giving me the space I needed.

"How'd I get here?" I inched my eyes around the office before landing on Rooster.

He held his hands up in front of him. "Don't look at me. I don't got that kind of focus. It was College Boy here that saved the day." He threw a thumb in the new ghost's direction.

"Thanks," I told him, swinging my legs over the side of the couch to sit up. The world spun on its axis, and I clutched the sides of the sofa to keep from tipping over.

"Woah, take it easy." A hand touched my shoulder, a very corporeal hand that sent a chill going through my clothes.

I blinked up at the ghost in the letterman's jacket. "How are you doing that?"

His lips quirked to one side. "Practice. You can call me Champ. Everyone else does." He shrugged a shoulder like it wasn't a big deal.

I nodded and then groaned, touching my head once more. "God, what I wouldn't do for some aspirin." An aspirin bottle shook in front of my face. I glanced over at Champ with a curious frown as I took the bottle out of his hand. "Thanks."

"No problem."

I found my water bottle on the coffee table in front of me and downed two of the pills. Sighing on the last gulp, I leaned back on the couch and stared at the two ghosts before me. "Not that I'm not grateful and all, but how come he can touch things, and you can't?" I pointed from Champ to Rooster. "Aren't you older than him?"

Rooster crooked a lopsided grin. "Not all of us spend our afterlife practicing with rocks." He gave Champ a sideways look, making Champ shuffle in place, his eyes down on the ground.

Arching a brow, I shook my head and winced again. I had to stop doing that. I sat up and thought about attempting to stand but wasn't quite ready for it. "Where's Shakespeare?"

"Shakespeare?" Champ asked. "Who's that?"

"You know, Ben," I explained, gesturing with my hand.

Rooster laughed, a full-throated laugh. "Oh God, that's a good one, toots. I'll have to remember that."

Champ huffed a laugh. "I suppose he does sound like he's just stepped out of Macbeth."

I gave him a look. "Macbeth? Really?"

"What? I can't read?"

I blushed. "No, I didn't mean to imply you couldn't. Just most guys go for Hamlet, not Macbeth."

This time, Champ blushed. He scratched the back of his head and scuffed his foot on the floor. "I don't know. I guess I relate to Macbeth. You know, doing something you shouldn't to get what you want?"

I huffed a laugh. "Macbeth murdered someone to become king and then ended up dead himself. I don't know if that's exactly a role model."

Champ shoved his hands into his pockets, his broad shoulders stiff. "I didn't say I idolized him, just that I could relate to him."

"Not to break up your little brain brash." Rooster sat on the edge of the couch and laced his fingers between his thighs. "We have more pressing matters at hand." He gestured two fingers at my head. "You might have a concussion." When I just stared at him, he sucked his teeth and shifted his cigarette from one side of his mouth to the other. "What? I can't know stuff? I might not have the jets like you two, but I'm not exactly a knob."

"Do you know what he's saying?" I asked Champ with an exasperated sigh.

Champ chuckled. "Nope. Half the ghosts here don't seem like they are even on the same wavelength, let alone speak English."

"Hey!" Rooster jerked to his feet, pulling his cigarette from his mouth to point at Champ. "You're cruisin' for a bruisin'. I speak English fine."

Champ and I exchanged a look and then burst out laughing. Rooster cursed at us until we stopped laughing before stomping off through the office wall right after flipping us the bird.

"So, about Ben?" I sagged back into the couch cushions. "What's at the creek?"

Champ clamped up faster than a nun's ass in a strip club. He cleared his throat and looked anywhere but at me. "You should really go get checked out at the ER. Do you have anyone who could come get you? You probably shouldn't be driving. Your mom?"

"She died when I was a kid."

"Oh, sorry." Champ visibly swallowed. "What about your dad?"

My eyes burned. I pushed it down. "No. No. He's gone too."

He breathed out a bitter laugh. "Man, I'm really stepping in it today." He watched me for a long moment, those blue eyes searching. "It was recently, wasn't it? Your dad?"

I nodded and turned my face away from the intensity of his eyes. "Yeah. A few weeks ago. Car accident."

There was a long pause before Champ said, "I'm sorry."

The way he said it made me look at him. There was some emotion in his face I couldn't decipher. I'd had a lot more sorrys in the last month than I could ever ask for. Champ's was nothing like any of the others. Empty words meant to make me go away and stop talking about it. Something you say just to feel good about yourself. Not Champ. He really seemed to actually mean it.

There was a long awkward pause between us before I licked my lips and broke it. "Uh, I have an aunt that's in town. I'll call her." I moved to get up, but Champ held a hand up. I watched him walk over to the desk and pick up my phone. The screen came on at his touch, and he stared down at the screen for a long time.

My screensaver was a picture of my dad and me at a Dolphin's game last year. We were both painted, and jersey'd to the nines. I knew the image well. It was one of the best memories I had of my dad.

I thought he might say something about it. When he handed the phone to me without a word, I didn't know what to say. Choosing to ignore his weirdness, I took it from him and said, "Thanks."

"Do you want me to wait with you until your aunt comes?"

Shaking my head slightly, for once not in pain, I pulled up my aunt's number. "No. Thanks though. You should probably go make sure Rooster doesn't cause a ruckus. Scaring some poor birds or something." I laughed lightly.

"Alright. If you're sure."

"I am." I interrupted him. I waited until Champ disappeared through the wall before pushing the send button.

It rang forever before my Aunt Christine's groggy voice came over the line. "Hello?"

"Hey, it's Braxton. Can you come pick me up?"

"Braxton, it's after two in the morning. Aren't you at work?" Her voice became more precise the more she spoke.

"Uh, yeah. I had a bit of an accident."

There was shuffling around and drawers shutting and opening. "What happened? I'm coming now."

"It's fine. Really. I just tripped and hit my head on a gravestone."

"A gravestone? Braxton, you could have a concussion. Bleeding in your brain," her breathing came out faster as she spoke, "I can't lose you too, Brax. I just can't."

MY SOUL TO TAKE

"Aunt Christine. Breath. I'm okay. It's not even bleeding anymore." I touched my forehead, making sure I wasn't lying. "I just want to be safe and go to the hospital."

"Okay. Okay. I'm fine. I'm coming. Just don't go to sleep. Okay? You have to stay awake." Her voice was taking on that panicked tone again. "I could stay on the phone and keep you up if you need me to."

"That won't be necessary." I grinned into the phone. "I need to call Edgar and let him know I'm leaving. I'll wait for you by the front gate."

"I'll be there in five minutes tops."

"Don't wreck to get to me, Aunt Christine." When there was silence on the other line, I repeated it sternly. "I mean it. I don't want to lose you too."

"You won't. I'll be careful. I'll see you soon." Her voice broke. "I love you."

"Love you too."

She finally hung up, and I could call Edgar. He told me to take care of myself and not to worry about the cemetery. It'd be okay for one night. I couldn't say for sure I agreed. The cemetery would be fine, sure, but what about the trespassers. Would they be fine, or would my ghostly friends cause all kinds of havoc while I was gone?

Chapter 9

I STOOD BY THE front gate, my hands shoved into my hoodie. Keeping my head down, I closed my eyes and tried to take deep, even breaths. Nausea had come with a vengeance.

"How are you fairing?"

I snorted, glancing over at Shakespeare. "About as good as someone with a likely concussion. It would be better if my stomach didn't want to come out of my throat."

Shakespeare stepped closer to me, his dark eyes peering into me. "My apologies for not being there for you before. I had other business that needed my attention."

"Yeah. Right. At the creek." I wrapped my arms around myself and squinted at him. "What's at the creek, Ben?"

MY SOUL TO TAKE

He gave me a small, sad smile. "Do not bother yourself with such things right now. Your health is all that matters. All else can wait."

"What if I don't want to wait?" I countered, getting annoyed by all the sidestepping of the conversation. "What if I want to know now?"

"Braxton, please. I beseech you."

"You beseech me?" I let out a hard laugh. "That's funny. You know this is my job. I'm the one who is supposed to be taking care of things here. Not you. You're just a ghost. You're not supposed to be here. When you die, you're supposed to go to the other side, not linger around and make the part timer's job a living hell. You're...you're..." I waved a hand at him, taking an angry step forward. "You're not even alive." It was a lame ending to my rampage. I blamed it on the concussion.

Ben stared at me for a long moment before inclining his head. "You are correct. Nothing you have said is in any way wrong. However, I am here. For as long as I am. And until the time comes that you are capable of dealing with what else lies within this world, regrettably I will have to hold my cards as they are to myself."

My foot moved forward one step. Before I could retort back, a blinding set of headlights poured over me through the gate. I put a hand up and peered out against the light. Aunt Christine.

"Braxton?" Her voice came from the rolled-down window.

I waved at her. "Can you cut the lights, please?"

"Oh, right." She turned the lights off but stayed in the car.

Turning back to Ben, I frowned. He was gone. Scowling out into the cemetery, I muttered, "Coward."

Picking my backpack up off the ground, I swung it over my shoulder and headed toward the gate. A brush of cold air touched the back of my neck, making me pause before I pushed through the metal entrance. Cursing under my breath about stupid pain in the ass ghosts and their constant need to be cryptic, I climbed into Aunt Christine's car.

"What do you have against Shakespeare?" Aunt Christine laughed, turning the lights back on. They glared into the cemetery, lighting up the distinct figure of Champ watching us.

Staring at him, I waited to see if Aunt Christine would notice him. When she looked straight through him and backed out of the driveway, it was clear she didn't see him like I did.

"Uh, nothing. We're just studying him in English class. He's being a pain in the ass." I leaned against the door, my forehead pressed up against the cold glass of the window.

MY SOUL TO TAKE

"I don't know. I always thought he was kind of hot." Aunt Christine grinned over at me.

My lips twitched. "You're such a freak."

"Hey, that's Madame Freak to you."

I snorted. "Yeah. Yeah. Just get me to the hospital without killing us, and I'll keep your dirty secret for Old Willy."

"Ooh. Old Willy. I like that." She bumped me with her elbow. "Have to remember to use that later."

"Oh, god. Please don't. I don't want to know."

All the way to the hospital, Aunt Christine kept talking my ear off, trying to gross me out as much as possible. At least, that's what it seemed like. I knew what she was really doing, though. I had to stay awake until the doctor said I was okay. No matter how much my head pounded or how much I wanted to just close my eyes and rest, I had to stay awake. There was no way I'd go to sleep with the images of my aunt doing the dirty with half the historical figures in any of my school books.

"Alright, here we are." Aunt Christine parked the car and turned to me. "Let's make sure your noggin isn't messed up. Well, more than it was before anyway."

"Thanks." I scoffed and climbed out of the car.

Once in the hospital's ER, I looked over the pitiful group of people waiting in the dingy blue chairs. Everyone here would have some reason or another; they had to be seen right then.

Mother with a sick baby. A dumb ass who'd no doubt cut himself doing something stupid on a dare. The list went on and on. I was only one of a dozen or more walking through those doors. I was sure the staff thought they had heard it all before.

Not my story.

Except I couldn't tell them the truth. That I'd fallen trying to hit a ghost. Nope. I'd have to tell them the saner person version that I'd told Aunt Christine.

"You fell at work?" the woman behind the desk asked, typing on her computer. "Do you need a report of your visit for workman's comp?"

I opened and shut my mouth. "Uh...I'm not sure. Can I get one just in case?"

"Sure. Go fill this out, and someone will call for you when it's time. Don't go to sleep." She gave me a stern look before waving me off.

I gave her a tight smile, holding my clipboard of paperwork to my chest.

"Want me to do that?" Aunt Christine reached for the papers.

"Oh, god. Please. Yes." I handed it to her and flopped into the chair next to her. "How long do you think this will take? I really want to just go to bed."

"Hard to say." She began filling out the papers. "One time, I waited for four hours just to get my finger sewn back on."

MY SOUL TO TAKE

"What?" I jerked up in my chair, staring at her. "What finger? Which one?"

She chuckled and wiggled her fingers at me. "Just making sure you're awake. It wasn't my fingers in any case, but I did get my shoulder knocked out of place once from trying to do this one karma sutra move, where you -"

"Lalalalala," I put my fingers in my ears and turned away from her. "I'm not hearing this."

Thankfully, it wasn't four hours of waiting— only about half an hour. By the time I got called back, another fresh batch of injured and broken had poured in.

"So, you tripped at work and hit your head on a gravestone?" the doctor repeated back to me my own story, his eyes looking over the glasses on his nose. "And you didn't pass out?" He peered at the cut on my forehead.

"Uh, no. Just jarred me a bit," I lied through my teeth, my eyes tightening in pain as he poked at the wound. "I got back to the office and called my aunt. She came and got me, and here we are."

"You're one lucky young lady," the doctor began, taking the cleaning cloths from the nurse at his side. "If you'd passed out, you might not have woken up again."

I hissed a sharp breath as he cleaned the wound. "Yeah. I'm lucky, alright."

When the doctor was done checking me over and announced I only had a mild concussion, he handed me a prescription for pain meds. "The stitches will dissolve on their own once it's healed. Take this down to the pharmacy. Take them as needed for your headache."

"Can I sleep?" I asked, desperate for my bed.

"I want you to go home and get some rest, but you'll need someone to wake you every few hours for the first twelve hours. Can someone stay with you tomorrow?"

"I can." My aunt raised her hand.

"But you have to go back to work?" I frowned at her.

She shrugged. "I'll call in. It's fine." She took the prescription from the doctor, leaving me no room to argue.

"Good." The doctor pushed his glasses up his nose. "Now, you need to take it easy. That means no work. I can write you a note if you need me to."

I shook my head. "No, that's okay. I think I'll be okay. My boss is pretty nice."

"Well, I'll give you one anyway." He scribbled something on his notepad and then ripped it off, handing it to Aunt Christine. "Make sure she rests."

"If I have to tie her to her bed, I will," she joked. When the doctor didn't laugh, she clucked her tongue and turned to me. "Well, okay. You ready, kiddo?"

"Yeah." I slid off the counter and followed her out of the examination room. We stopped by the pharmacy to get meds and then piled back into the car. The sun was just coloring the horizon pink when we finally parked in the driveway. I climbed painstakingly into the house and up to my bedroom. Aunt Christine brought up the rear, stopping to get me a glass of water.

Shoving my shoes off, I changed into my PJs and climbed under the blankets. Aunt Christine pulled a chair up beside my bed and handed me the water and pills. When I was done, I passed it back to her.

"You don't have to stay in here with me," I told her as she settled in next to my bed. "You can just set the alarm and go back to bed or watch tv or something."

"Nah, I've got my book here." She lifted a paperback up with a shirtless man and a woman with the top half of her dress torn. "I'll read for a bit then wake you up. I may do some work calls once the regular people are up and walking about." She grinned at me and tapped my covered legs with her book. "Get some sleep. You earned it."

I settled back into my pillows and let my eyes droop. I didn't know if I deserved it, but I knew I needed it. I thought it would take longer to fall asleep. As if the events of this weekend would keep me awake, but one moment I was awake, and the next I was gone. So much for self-control.

Chapter 10

IT WAS ACTUALLY A relief to have a break from the cemetery Sunday night. After Aunt Christine woke me up every few hours as the doctor instructed, we spent the rest of the day binging bad television dramas and eating junk food. Sure, it wasn't the most productive day, but it beat the hell out of getting my head bashed in some more.

"So..." Aunt Christine trailed off, looking to me in between commercial breaks. She bit off some licorice and raised her brows at me. "School tomorrow? How ya feeling about that?"

I scoffed. "Way to be subtle." Grabbing a handful of chocolate-covered raisins, I popped a few into my mouth while I thought of an answer.

MY SOUL TO TAKE

Aunt Christine shoved my knees with her foot next to me on the couch. "Come on, don't hold it all in. It's not good for your health."

Grimacing, I touched my forehead. "Yeah, and neither are tombstones."

She grunted a laugh at that. Unfortunately, she kept watching me until I finally sighed and threw down my snacks.

"Fine. I'm a bit anxious."

"Only a bit?"

I shrugged and hugged my knees. "I know exactly what's going to happen tomorrow. I'll go to class, everyone will either avoid me like the plague or make fake small talk with a lot, 'of how are you doing's? We're so sorry for your loss. You're so brave to come back so soon.' On and on." I waved a hand in the air and leaned back against the couch. "I'd rather be working, to be honest."

Aunt Christine's warm hand landed on mine. She squeezed it slightly. "I understand. It's going to be hard for a while. And while they mean well, people just don't know what to say, but hey, at least they're trying? You have to give them credit for that."

"Yeah. I guess." I blew out a hard breath. "I just wish I could skip to the end, you know? To the part where they forget it happened and just act normal. That's what I need right now. Normal." And for ghosts to stop talking to me.

That part, I kept to myself. I didn't need my aunt thinking my head injury was worse than it was.

"Don't worry. It will get better. It just takes time. Besides, if you quit now, what will you do with the rest of your life? Work in the cemetery?" She laughed before turning back toward the television.

I thought about what she said for a while as I chewed on my snacks. Working at the cemetery for the rest of my life didn't seem so bad. It was a pretty cushy job if you didn't mind the dark or well, ghosts.

One ghost, in particular, came to mind. Shakespeare. Ben.

I'd been such a bitch to him this morning. Sure, I could have lopped it in with the concussion, but really I was just angry they were keeping things from me. I was the one that was in charge. Not them. What was so special about this creek anyway?

Edgar had asked me to stay away from it. Animals, he'd said. Pfft. I didn't believe that for one second. If the ghosts were interested in what was going on over there, then it had to be more than just wild animals.

I had to figure out what was going on there. Plus, apologize to Ben. I grimaced. That was not going to be pleasant. Though, I expect he would be far more forgiving than any of the living. After all, I was the only one who could see him. What choice did he have?

MY SOUL TO TAKE

Sunday was gone quicker than I would have liked, and Monday's morning light came pouring through my windows. I groaned and put my pillow over my head, wanting nothing more than to go back to sleep and not face the onslaught of questions and condolences that were sure to come my way.

Finally, I forced myself out of bed, dragging my feet the whole way. I showered and dressed, making sure to artfully cover my wound with my hair. I didn't need more stares than I was already going to get.

I could hear Aunt Christine downstairs talking on the phone as I made my way down the steps. Walking into the kitchen, I found her sitting on the counter with an annoyed expression on her face. I waved to her with a tight smile. She rolled her eyes and pointed at the phone, mimicking talking with her hand.

Pulling the fridge open, I grabbed a bottle of water and then an apple from the counter. I waved at my aunt before heading out the door, snatching up my backpack on the way out.

Once in my car, I sagged in my seat and sighed. Today was going to be one long day.

I blared music all the way to school, trying to keep my head focused on it and not on what was waiting for me at my first class and most likely at every class that day. Unfortunately, my first encounter didn't wait until I was in my classroom. It was waiting for me in the common room.

"Braxton, you showed up!" Mandy practically squealed before she wrapped her arms around me in a tight hug. Pulling back, she held me by the shoulders. "I'm so glad you came. I was telling everyone that I was sure you'd show up because you said you would. But don't worry, it won't be weird. I told everyone to just be cool. So don't worry, okay?"

"Okay," I forced a smile.

She grinned back a bit more brightly than needed and hugged me again. "Oh, I'm so happy to see you. I missed you."

"I missed you too," I replied because that was what she wanted. Honestly, I was too much in my own head to miss anyone but my dad. I couldn't say that to her, though. I wasn't a total bitch.

So, I let Mandy loop her arm in mine and lead me to our first class together. Econ 204. I hated this class: so much theology and hard thinking. Give me a book to read and a report to write any day.

True to her word, not a single person bombarded me with questions or condolences. Though I did get a few sideways looks of pity, Mandy quickly stopped those with a firm look. She encouraged me to sit with her in our regular seats, front, and center of the class. Had it not been for Mandy, I would have chosen to sit in the

MY SOUL TO TAKE

back, where I could slouch down and pretend to be invisible. This close up, it was inviting people to stare.

"It's okay," Mandy squeezed my hand. "I've got you."

I nodded stiffly and waited for the professor to arrive.

Professor Norton walked through the door a few minutes later, his tweed jacket a pukey green today and his plaid sweater vest a mix match of greens and reds as if he couldn't wait for Christmas to come. Once he set his briefcase down and moved around his desk, his eyes scanned the room.

I tried to make myself as small as possible. That was hard to do when you were in the front row. So, when Professor Norton's eyes landed on me, I looked straight back at him.

"I hope you all had a good weekend," he began, his eyes drifting away from me once more. I relaxed in my seat. Maybe he wouldn't single me out. "I'm glad to see so many faces so bright and early on a Monday morning. And a face that had been dearly missed." His gaze settled back on me. Fuck. "Our condolences, Miss Clay, for your loss. I'm sure you want nothing more than to get back to normal, and so without further ado, a pop quiz!"

The class groaned as he pulled a pile of papers out of his bag and handed them down the rows.

Great. Not only did he point me out as the sad girl in class, but now everyone would be mad at me for making them take a quiz this early in the week.

When the papers came to me, Professor Norton stopped before my desk. "Now, I'm sure you've been doing your best to make up what you've missed, but try not to let this quiz stress you out. It's only to see what everyone is retaining. It won't hurt your final grade." He offered me a reassuring smile that I strained to return.

One good thing about the quiz was that it forced everyone to pay attention to the test and not me. No whispers or questions were being asked. Only the ones on the paper. Ones that I only about half knew the answers to, which wasn't much different from any other quiz in that class.

Finally, Econ was over, and I could go on to a more enjoyable class. One that didn't have - Mandy-

"Hey, Braxton! Wait up!"

I tried to pretend I didn't hear her. Not sure if I could fake anymore bubbly excitement, but she didn't have long legs for nothing. Mandy caught up to me in no time.

"Hey Mandy." I pretended to be happy to see her. "I didn't hear you there."

"No worries." She waved me off with a breeze of her hand. "So, I wanted to see if you want to go to Bonnie's after class? Get a milkshake? You know, like we used to."

"Oh, um." I immediately wanted to say no. I'd much rather curl up at home and focus on my school work than spend my free time gossiping with her at Bonnie's. Except I was supposed to be trying to get back to normal. This was what I would typically do. So, I had to go. "Yeah. Sure. Sounds good."

Once I saw how excited she was, I was happy to have said yes.

"Great!" Mandy practically skipped in place. "I'll see you then. Three o'clock. Don't be late."

I watched her leave and rubbed my face with a sigh. Wincing when my fingers found my cut, I dropped my hand: one class down, one to go.

Walking toward my next class, Calculus the bane of my existence, I had my mind all set on doing equations until my brain split open when I bumped into a firm body. I opened my mouth to apologize as I lifted my head up but clamped it shut when I saw who it was.

"Dean," I clipped his name out with an irritated scowl. From his black loafers to his polo shirt, Dean was everything that was wrong and privileged with the world. Why he hadn't gone to Hill Valley instead of Richmond, I'd never know.

"Whatever you have to say, save it. I need to go to class." I tried to sidestep him. He just moved in front of me.

"Look, I just want to apologize, and you know, offer my condolences." he offered with a small smile. "Maybe a shoulder to cry on?"

"Ugh," I pushed past him. "You're unbelievable, you know that?"

"Hey, come on now." Dean came up beside me, not taking a hint. "I said I was sorry. I didn't know you're dad had just died, or I would have - "

"You would have what, Dean?" I spun around on him, glowering at him. "You'd have waited until after the funeral to try and assault me?"

Dean scowled, grabbing my arm and pulling me close as he harshly whispered, "You were into it until you started crying and saying no. How was I supposed to know you were being serious?"

"Maybe by the words coming out of my mouth, asshole." I swung my bag around and smacked him with it until he turned me loose. "Don't touch me. Don't talk to me. Ever again. Or I will report you to the school."

"This isn't over, Braxton," Dean called after me. "Not by a long shot."

I flipped him off and ducked into Calculus. I'd been right the first time. This was going to be a long-ass fucking day.

Chapter 11

THE REST OF SCHOOL passed by pretty quickly. I didn't get away from getting a handful of condolences and how are you doings, but it was bearable. Tomorrow would be better. It had to be.

I was actually happy to see Mandy when three o'clock came around, and I walked into Bonnie's. She was already sitting at our regular booth off to the side and toward the back. Her blonde hair cascading around her face as she stared down at her phone. Her eyes lifted as I approached, and a smile lit her face.

"Braxton," she beamed. "I don't know why I keep expecting you not to show up, but here you are again."

"Yeah," I breathed out, sinking into my side of the booth. "Here I am."

She waved the waitress over, who took our orders—two chocolate milkshakes with the whip cream on the bottom. Once the waitress was gone, Braxton grabbed my hands and leaned forward.

"Tell me, truthfully, how was it?"

I slid down the booth seat and glanced off to the side. "It wasn't so bad except for..." I trailed off, not knowing if I should talk about Dean. I'd told Mandy what he had done right after it had happened, but I still felt guilty. Mandy had always had a thing for him, and the fact that I had even done anything with him, let alone the fact that he turned out to be such an asshole, made me feel like such a bad friend.

"What? Braxton, you can tell me anything."

I grimaced and then finally gave in. "Dean was giving me a hard time, is all."

She made a face, her nose all scrunched up and her tongue wagging like it had left a bad taste in her mouth. "Ew. Dean. Seriously. I don't know what I ever saw in that guy. I'm so sorry you had to face him alone. I'd have walked you, but my class was all the way on the other side of the building."

"I know. It's fine," I reassured her.

We paused our talking while the waitress placed down our milkshakes. When she was gone, Mandy leaned in and said in a conspiring voice, "You know what we should do?"

MY SOUL TO TAKE

"What?" I asked, taking a long drag of my shake. The cold liquid slid down my throat, reminding me too much of the ghosts back at the cemetery. Great. They'd ruined even milkshakes for me.

"We should teach Dean a lesson. You know, fill his car with slime or take him to the woods, strip him naked and leave him there. Or-"

"Scare the crap out of him with ghosts?" I proposed only half-joking.

Mandy looked at me for a second, and then her lips curled up into a mischievous grin. "That's it. That's perfect! You can tell him you want to give him a second chance. Have him meet you at the cemetery, and then I can make all kinds of crazy stuff happen. Really freak him out, you know?"

"Uh, I was only kidding." Shit. Shit. Shit. "Besides, I don't think Dean will believe I want to give him another chance after today's conversation."

She waved me off, thinking. "He's a guy. He'll come if there's any chance for him to hook up. The problem is Old Man Edgar. If he catches us, he'll call the cops on our asses."

I scratched the back of my head and shifted in my seat. "Uh, yeah. About that. I think I can take care of that."

"What do you mean?" She sipped her drink, eyes on me.

"I kind of took a part-time job as the weekend groundskeeper at the cemetery."

"You what?" Mandy shouted, causing all the other guests to stare at us. Lowering her voice, she pushed her shake to the side and grabbed my hands. "Why didn't you tell me you got a job? And a creepy-ass one like that? You could have gotten a job at the Gap with me or something. Plus, now you've lost all your weekends."

I shrugged. "It's not too bad. Pretty relaxing, actually." If you don't mind the ghosts pestering you all the time.

Mandy gave me that pitying look that meant I wouldn't like the next thing she said. "Braxton, honey. You didn't get this job because of your dad, did you?"

Pulling my hands out of hers, I wrapped them around my drink, twisting it around in my hands. "Partly. Look," I huffed at her look of pity. "I needed to find a job anyway—this one kind of fell into my lap. While the hours might sucky, the pay is great, and I get dental! Besides, I got to scare the shit out of some frat guys from Richmond. Can't get better than that."

"Okay," she drew out, sitting back in her seat. "If you're sure."

"I am."

"Good."

We were quiet for a moment, and then Mandy leaned forward again. "So, Friday night. You, Dean, and the undead. What do you say?"

I groaned and covered my face with my hand. "Fine. Fine. I know I'm going to regret this but let's do it."

"Yes!" She pumped her arms at her side and then went on to explain all her ideas for freaking Dean out. She wanted him to cry like a little baby or maybe even wet his pants in fear. While Mandy said this was all about me, I had a feeling some of it was for her too. Dean had been her crush for a long time, and he'd kind of destroyed that pedestal she had put him on by attacking me. So, even though I just wanted to put the whole thing behind me, if this was what Mandy needed, who was I to say no?

"Hey, Brax?" Aunt Christine called up the stairs the next day. "I'm leaving. You gonna come say goodbye?"

"Yeah, hold on a second." I put my pencil down on my Calculus book and headed down the stairs.

Aunt Christine stood by the back door, her coat and purse already on. She held her arms out, and I eagerly went into her waiting embrace.

"I'm sorry you missed work because of me," I muttered into her coat. "I'm going to miss you."

"Don't you worry about me. Family comes first. Always." She hugged me tightly and kissed me on the head. "Now, don't go getting into any trouble while I'm gone. I'm running out of vacation time." She brushed my hair away from my forehead, looking at my healing wound. "Try to save your next injury for a holiday, will ya?"

I chuckled. "I'll try. Be safe on the road."

"I will be." She squeezed me in her arms one more time before releasing me. "I love you, Braxton. Keep your chin up. Things will get better. Okay?"

I nodded. "Okay."

My eyes trailed after my aunt as she climbed into her car and pulled out of the driveway. I watched her all the way until her taillights were gone down the street before I finally turned back to the house.

It seemed so empty and lonely without Aunt Christine here. Unbearable.

Nope. I wasn't doing this.

I grabbed my keys and shoved my feet into my tennis shoes. Walking purposely to my dad's car, Aunt Christine had taken me back to get it from the cemetery the other day. I slid into the driver seat and cranked the car. The music blared over the speakers as I pulled out of the driveway and onto the road. I didn't know where I was going, but I wasn't staying home. Nope. I was done with moping about things. I needed to do something. Eat something. Anything.

There was no explanation of how it happened. One minute I was driving down the road thinking of burgers and fries, and then next, I was pulling up to the cemetery gates. It was barely past five o'clock. The sun hadn't even set yet. Hopefully, that meant that the ghosts wouldn't come out to play, and I could visit my dad in peace.

Walking down the gravel path, I tucked my hands into my hoodie and kept my eyes down. Maybe if I didn't make eye contact, they wouldn't bother me. That was the hope anyway.

As luck would have it, I made it to my dad's grave without running into Edgar or any ghosts.

I placed my hand on top of his gravestone and smiled a watery smile. "Hey, Dad. It's been a few days. I went back to school this week." I took a deep breath and sank down onto the ground before the grave, my legs up in front of me. I leaned my arms on my legs and told him all the things that had happened this week. "Mandy wants to get back at Dean. Heh. I just want to put it all behind me. He's not worth the waste of time and energy."

"Aunt Christine went home today, and the house feels, well, it feels so empty without you. I know it's been a few weeks since you passed, but it still feels like yesterday." I rubbed my chest with my fist. "There's this hole in my chest that just won't go away. And everyone keeps telling me everything is going to be okay. That it will get better. But when? When will it? Cause right now, I didn't see the light at the end of the tunnel. All I saw was pain and loneliness in the future. If I even have one." I sucked in a shuddering breath and leaned my face onto my hands.

After a few minutes, I lifted my head to find my three ghostly companions standing before me. Rooster, with his cigarette, pinched tightly between his lips. Champ with his hands shoved into his pockets like most of our generation did when trying to not be obvious. Then there was Shakespeare. Ben. He openly watched me without a hint of remorse at having seen me cry.

"Here," Ben knelt before me and held out a handkerchief.

I arched a brow. "I don't think that's going to help me much."

"Do you have to make everything a brawl?" Ben gestured the handkerchief at me again. "Just take the damnable thing."

Sighing but knowing what was going to happen. I reached out and waited for my fingers to go through the cloth. When they didn't, I let out a surprised, "oh." Staring at Ben in wonder, I pulled the handkerchief to my face and wiped my eyes.

"I've been practicing," Ben told my questioning gaze. His eyes glanced over to Champ and Rooster. "Would you gentlemen give the lady and me a few moments alone?"

Rooster took the cigarette out of his mouth and shoved it behind his ear as he nodded and then disappeared.

Champ gave me one more surveying look before he walked away, leaving Ben and me alone.

"How are you fairing?" Ben asked, lifting a ghostly hand to my forehead. His cool touch brushed my hair to the side but didn't cause my injury any pain.

Shrugging a shoulder, I leaned back from his touch. "As well as can be expected. I only had a mild concussion. I took some pills for the pain, and that's it. I'll be fine."

Ben gave me a small smile. "Now who is being cryptic? That was not exactly my meaning."

"Oh." I glanced off to the side, trying to ignore the intensity of his gaze. "I'm sorry for what I said the other night," I blurted out, changing the subject.

"The other night?" Ben arched a brow at me, still kneeling at my side. "I do not know what you speak of."

"When I yelled at you," I reminded him, pushing to my knees, so I wasn't at such a disadvantage.

"Oh," Ben smiled. "That. I do not blame the lady for being perturbed. You were injured. It is only natural to lash out at others."

"That's no excuse," I argued, shaking my head. "I shouldn't have yelled at you like that. You might be dead, but that doesn't mean I can treat you that way."

Ben stared at me, bemused. "I cannot figure you out, Braxton Clay. There are so many layers to you. I find myself drowning in the pure complexity of your essence."

I blushed. "You make me sound like this big deep person when I'm not. I'm just me."

"Still," Ben came closer to me, his eyes bore into me, making my skin feel hot and tight. "I deeply wish I had known you while I was alive."

"Why?" I murmured, not sure why I lowered my voice.

"So, I could do this."

Ben lowered his face toward mine, and though it was ridiculous, I did nothing to stop it. Frozen in place, I felt the brush of his cold lips against mine, barely a touch at all, really. More like an itch? I didn't know, but when it was over, I found myself disappointed and wanting more.

"Braxton? Is that you?"

My eyes shot open, and my head jerked toward Edgar's voice. "Uh, yeah. It's me."

"What are you doing over there messing with that ghost?"

My eyes widened as I scrambled to my feet, gesturing to Ben with urgency. "You can see him?"

Chapter 12

"WHAT DO YOU MEAN, can I see him?" Edgar shuffled toward me with a furrowed brow. "Of course, I can. You think I don't know what goes on in my own cemetery."

"I thought I was the only one," I stammered, glancing between Edgar and Ben, still not believing this was happening.

"Nope," Edgar answered, narrowing his eyes on Ben. "What in the world do you think you are doing, Benedick? She's a live girl. You're a ghost. You shouldn't be leading her on like that."

Ben had the decency to look contrite as he took his lashings. "My apologies, Edgar. The lady was in distress. I only wished to distract her from it."

I stared at Ben, not sure what I thought of his words.

"Well, you better get on now. I hear that new one is trying it again down by the creek." Edgar jerked his head toward the other side of the cemetery.

"Of course, of course." Ben nodded and gave me one final look before turning away and disappearing.

Left alone with Edgar, I suddenly felt exposed. Naked and not in a good way.

"Well, come on. Let's go inside." Edgar pivoted and headed back to the office with me on his tail.

When we arrived inside, I barely sat down before I blurted out, "Why didn't you tell me there were ghosts here?"

Edgar snorted, sitting his coffee cup down on the table before us. "Would you have taken the job? Or even believed me?"

"Well...no," I agreed reluctantly. "but it would have been nice to know. Nice to know I wasn't going crazy." I dragged a hand across my hair and down my ponytail before locking my gaze on Edgar. "So, you can talk to ghosts too. Anyone else?"

He shrugged a shoulder. "Not anyone else as far as I know."

I snorted. "Why are we so lucky? Why not someone else? Anyone else?"

"It's not like you win the lottery or picked it up at the grocery store. No one knows how or why. We just do." Edgar held his hands out to his sides, his gaze firmly on me.

"And what about the creek?"

His shoulders stiffened at my question. "The creek is just what I said, dangerous. Keep away from it."

I frowned, my brows drawn together. "Fine. Apparently, I can handle the ghosts, but I can't handle anything else. Not like they're going to tell me anyway." I'd have to figure it out myself, it seemed. The first chance I had, I would find this mysterious creek and figure out what the hell is so special about it.

"And don't you be getting any ideas!" Edgar waved a finger at me sternly. "I'd hate to lose you after you just got hired on."

I blew air out between my teeth. "Thanks. Nice to know where I stand."

"Now, it ain't like that, young lady, and you know it. But you better stay away from that creek if you know what's good for you. While you're at it, keep away from those ghosts. Ben is a smooth talker that one, but he's a ghost, and you need to remember that. You hear?"

My lips twisted to the side. "I don't know what you're talking about."

"That Rooster ain't no better." Edgar continued as if I hadn't even spoken. "He'd ride you hard and put you up wet. That's if he could touch you. Which thank your lucky stars he can't."

I snorted, not believing half of what he was saying. "You gonna tell me Champ is bad news too?"

Edgar's brows rose to his hairline. "Champ?

"Yeah, you know." I sat up straight and waved a hand over my body. "College boy. Wears a letterman's jacket. Sad puppy dog eyes."

Edgar shook his head. "I don't know any Champ, but I'd stay away from him either way."

I huffed. "How exactly am I going to do that? They aren't exactly easy to ignore."

"Well, practice. Do your job and stay out of trouble. That's all you have to do." He sighed and pushed to his feet by his hands on his knees. Something cracked, and he groaned. "Now you say your piece to your dad and head on home. I'll be closing the gates shortly."

Seeing as I wasn't going to get any more out of him, I followed Edgar out of the office and started toward my dad's grave. While the warning had been annoying, it did give me a lot to think about.

My tennis shoes crunched on the fallen leaves as I came off the path and over to my dad's grave. I knelt before it and placed my hand on top of the cold stone. "Hey, dad. Sorry about the interruption earlier. I had to get my ear chewed off by my boss." I chuckled, turning my head to one side. "He kind of reminds me of you a little bit. Knew I had all kinds of ideas rolling around in my head without me even saying so."

I sighed heavily and patted the stone. "Well, I just wanted to see you. It's been a tough week, and it's not getting any easier. I'll see ya around. I love you, Daddy." My eyes misted, and I swiped at the tears before they could fall.

Turning back up the path, I caught sight of Edgar at the gate with a woman and a little girl. The woman was around my age with long dark brown hair and a jean jacket. She held the strap of her purse tightly in one hand and the little girl's hand in the other. The little girl couldn't have been more than five with light brown hair curled at her shoulders. Her big brown eyes stared up at Edgar as he tried to usher them away.

"I'm sorry, but cemetery visiting hours are over. You'll have to come back in the morning."

I stepped closer, watching the interaction.

"But," the woman licked her lips and glanced down at the little girl, desperation on her face. "Can't you make an exception? This once? I don't get off work in time to get here during visiting hours, and Lucy has to be in school before I have to go to work. She just wants to see her dad."

Edgar stared at them for a long moment, and I could see the struggle on his expression. I couldn't imagine having to turn away a grieving child and mother because of some city ordinance. Wait. I guess that would be part of my job now too. Though, I probably will have less of that issue on the night shift.

"I understand your situation, but I really cannot make an exception for someone who does not work here. It's an insurance thing. You understand?" Edgar swept an arm out the gate, gesturing for them to leave.

I hurried across the path to catch up to them. "Hold on a sec, Edgar." I huffed and came to a jolting stop. "They're with me."

The woman stared at me in confusion while the child stared with fascination.

Edgar crossed his arms behind his back and slowly turned toward me, his brows raised. "Is that right, Braxton? Do you know these two?"

"Oh, yeah. We go way back, I asked..." I stared at the woman pointedly.

"Bianca."

"I asked Bianca to meet me here." I stepped between the two and Edgar. "I wanted to show them where I worked before my next shift."

Edgar watched our exchange closely, and I was pretty sure he didn't believe me for even a second. However, he sighed and shook his head. "Very well. You have ten minutes. Then they have to go." He shifted to leave before giving me a knowing look. "But you're responsible for them. If anything happens, it's on you."

I jerked my head in a nod. "Got it."

Pivoting to the two of them, I swept my arm forward and smiled. "You heard him. We've got ten minutes. Let's go check out some graves."

MY SOUL TO TAKE

Bianca didn't have to be told twice as she hurried after me, her little girl tightly at her side.

Once we were out of hearing distance, she murmured, "Thank you. You don't know how much this means to us. To her."

I gave her a small smile. "Don't mention it." I paused at a line of graves and rocked on my heels, my hands in my pockets. "So, where to?"

"Oh!" Bianca realized I had no idea where we were going and took the lead. "This way."

We walked down the path a little bit with the little girl looking back at me every few seconds. I smiled at the girl, which made her give me a big snaggle tooth smile back. We stopped a few graves later.

"This is it," Bianca announced.

I took a step back. "I'll give you your privacy." I turned my back on them and watched the trees around us, pretending I couldn't hear every word they were saying.

"Go ahead, Penny. It's okay." Bianca's voice was low, and encouraging to what I assumed was the little girl.

"What do I say, mommy?" her little voice, so sweet and innocent, made my eyes burn again. I sniffed and forced myself to keep it together.

"Whatever you want, baby. You want me to go first?" I guess Penny nodded because Bianca continued, "Hey, sorry it's taken so long to get out here. Work and school, you know how it is." She gave a nervous laugh. "The house isn't the same without you. Neither is school." Bianca paused and sniffed. "I really miss you, Champ."

Champ! These people were here for Champ? Shit.

I searched around the cemetery, scanning for any sign of the ghost that belonged to these two. A brush of leaves and a shadow hid in the trees. My eyes narrowed, trying to make out the figure. Was it, Champ? Why didn't he come out?

Not wanting to freak the two out, I kept my thoughts to myself and waited. I'd have to ask Champ later.

"Okay, Penny, your turn." I glanced back to see Bianca nudge the girl forward.

Penny shuffled across the grass, her head down and her hands tight at her side. "Daddy, it's me. Penny. I... I miss you. And uh, I wish you were here instead of in heaven with Grammy and Papa." She paused, and there was some shuffling before she spoke again. "I wanted to ask if you could find Mr. Snuggles. I left him at your house, but mommy says we can't go back there right now."

Bianca made a sound in her throat as if she wanted to say something about what Penny was saying but didn't want to stop Penny from talking to her dad.

"Uh, I don't know what else to say, mommy?"

"That's okay. You can come back another time if you want if you think of something else to say to Daddy." Bianca's voice turned to me. "We're done. Thank you. So much."

I twisted around and inclined my head. "No problem. I'm happy I could help." I took a step closer to them and looked down at Penny. Kneeling down to her level, I met her innocent gaze. "You know, I lost my dad too, just recently actually. I know it's confusing, and there will be times you just want him to be there again."

"Yeah," Penny said softly.

"You know what I do when I miss him?" I smiled at her. "I try to remember the good times we had. Because they're a part of us now. You know?"

"They are?" Penny cocked her head to the side, her little mouth pushed together.

"Yeah, right here," I pointed at her head and then her heart, "And here. You don't have to be at a grave to talk to him. He'll hear you as long as you keep him in your memories and your heart. Can you do that?"

Penny nodded eagerly. "I can do that."

"He was a lucky guy then to have a kid like you," I told her, standing. I met Bianca's gaze and suddenly felt guilty. Rubbing the back of my neck, I grimaced. "Sorry, I hope I didn't overstep my boundaries..."

"No, no." Bianca waved me off, taking Penny's hand with a small tilt of her lips. "I liked what you said. Thank you. Well, for everything." She glanced off past me before adding on, "We better get out of here before you get in trouble."

I looked behind me and didn't see anything. I shrugged. "Nah, don't worry about it. I work the night shift on the weekends. If you ever want to come by after hours, just let me know."

Bianca's eyes watered as she bobbed her head. "I will. Come on, baby. Let's get you home."

"Bye, Penny." I waved after the little girl, who shook her little hand back at me.

When they were gone, I turned back to the grave in front of me. The sun had mostly set, but I could just make out the tombstone. I frowned and took another step forward. My brows furrowed as I made out the name on the stone.

Peyton Rider.

Chapter 13

I GAPED AND SHOOK my head, not able to believe it. Champ? Champ was Peyton Rider? Sweet and caring Champ? It couldn't be.

Stumbling back from the grave, I spun around, my eyes searching for the figure in the shadows. When I found him, hiding out in the trees, I shouted, "You? That's you? You're Peyton Rider?"

Champ shrugged his shoulders.

"No, don't give me that noncommittal bullshit." I stomped toward the shadows wishing I could reach out and wring his incorporeal neck. "Here you've been walking around being nice to me, acting like nothing's wrong when it was *you*. You are the one who ruined my life. Who took my dad away from me!" I grabbed at his form, letting out a snarl of frustration when my fingers went right through him.

"Say something, damn it!" I stomped my foot and punched at his transparent body. Each hit went straight through him, but he just took it. He stood there without a word and let me wail on his ghostly form.

"Man, Doll Face. You've really flipped your wig this time."

"Not now, Rooster," I called over my shoulder and kept swinging at Champ, hoping with all I could that one, just one hit, would land on him.

Rooster chuckled and moved around me to stand beside us. "I get ya. You got beef with Champ, and you want to get even. But you ain't gonna do it that way."

I scowled and dropped my arms. Looking away from Champ for one moment, breathing heavily. "What are you talking about?"

"Yes, Rooster, please regale us with your wondrous thought process."

Great. Shakespeare had to show up now.

"Why don't you all just mind your own business and leave *Champ* and me here to settle our differences?" I snarled at the frat boy ghost who had yet to do anything to defend himself.

"Pfft. Differences, eh?" Rooster arched a brow at me, shifting his cigarette from one side of his mouth to the other. "More like attacking a poor fella who's already beating himself up for his choices," he waved a hand at Champ. "Can't you see the poor shmuck is torn up about it?"

That was when I really looked at Champ, or rather Rider. His hand shoved into the pockets of his letterman's jacket that now I recognized from Richmond College. Rider's shoulders weren't stiff in defense against my attacks. Still, they curled into himself as if he wanted to make himself as small as possible. My eyes lifted to his face, where I expected to see anger or at least annoyance at my actions. What I didn't expect was the deep despair and regret in every inch of his face.

I shifted in place, uncomfortable with the intensity of his grief.

Jerking my head to the side, so I didn't have to look at him anymore, I crossed my arms over my chest and sniffed. "Look, I get it. You've got a little girl. You lost someone. I lost someone."

Rider stepped forward and opened his mouth but I beat him to the punch.

I skittered back, a hand up between us. "I don't want to hear it."

"Braxton," Rider tried anyway. "I just...please...let me."

Shaking my head, I stared down at the ground and walked back quickly. "Nope. No. I'm not doing this. Not today." I lifted my hands and finally lifted my gaze to Rider's. For a second, just a brief second, I could see right into his soul, which was funny since I was pretty sure that's what his ghostly form was, but I didn't know what else to call it. What I did know was that it made me swallow a large lump in my throat as I shook my head again. "I've...I've gotta go."

I pivoted on my heel and didn't look back as I practically ran to my dad's car. Edgar stepped out of the office as I passed by, and I waved at him with a tight smile. Thankfully, he didn't try to stop me, and I made it to my car without another ghostly encounter.

On the way home, I drove through the burger joint and got my usual, except by the time I got home, I was so not hungry. I dropped the greasy bag of food on the counter and stalked through the house and up the stairs. I didn't stop until I reached the bathroom.

Stripping my hoodie off and then the rest of my clothes, I turned the water on until it was as hot as I could stand it. Then I stepped into the shower. The heat beat down on my skin like burning needles. I didn't mind. It took my thoughts off of what I'd learned. Off the anger building inside of me demanding me to go back and give Rider a piece of my mind. Exorcise him or something.

Why did he get to be a ghost and not my dad?

It wasn't fair.

I slapped the wall with my hand. It wasn't enough. I curled my fingers into a fist and punched the tiled wall as hard as I could. Pain radiated up my hand, and it felt...good. I hit the wall a few more times in rapid succession until my insides didn't feel so full, and I collapsed onto the shower floor.

Sobs wracked my body as I held my aching hand to my chest. I didn't know how long I sat there crying. It was long enough that the scalding hot water turned ice cold.

When I was shivering, I forced myself to climb out of the shower. I pulled the nearby hanging towel down, wrapped it around myself, and sat on the floor mat, my knees up to my chest.

My body and mind quieted, and all that was left was an overwhelming heaviness. My eyes lulled as I crawled to my feet. I dragged my hand along the wall, bracing myself as I made my way to my bed. Without getting dressed, I fell onto the bed, towel and all. Dragging the covers up and over my shoulders, I let myself be sucked down into the abyss.

Chapter 14

SCHOOL WENT BY IN a blur. Mandy was a constant by my side. Except when she had other classes, of course. Dean hadn't come back up to me again.

Part of me was relieved.

I didn't want to bring up old feelings again. I had enough going on in my life than to add him back to the mix. Unfortunately, Mandy wouldn't let me forget it.

"So, did you ask him?" she prodded on Friday morning, an over-eager look in her eyes.

I glanced up from my book in Econ and shook my head. "No. I haven't seen him."

Mandy scoffed. "He's not going to come to you. You have to go to him. Do you still have his number?"

I shrugged. "Yeah. I guess." Mainly so I knew who to avoid when they called.

"Then message him," Mandy hissed as the professor walked in the door.

"I don't know, Mandy. What would I even say?"

"Here," Mandy snatched my phone from my desk and scrolled through my contacts. Her fingers moved across the screen faster than I'd ever seen her type. She must really want this. Which was the only reason I wasn't stopping her.

Sometimes we just need someone to blame. Someone to punish. I knew that as well as anyone.

"There, done." Mandy handed my phone back to me.

I frowned as I looked at the text she sent.

I'm so sorry, Dean. I was overdramatic. Can I make it up to you?

"Mandy," I began to say with a sigh. I didn't get any more out because the professor started talking. All through class, I had to sit there anxious to talk to Mandy and even more worried about Dean's reply.

About the last five minutes of class, my phone buzzed. I glanced down at it discreetly. It was Dean.

I knew you'd come around. What'd you have in mind?

"What'd he say?" Mandy whispered quickly. "Come on, I'm dying here."

I blew out a breath and slid the phone across the desk so she could see it.

Thankfully, class was dismissed right as Mandy let out a squeal. "I knew he couldn't resist. What should we say now?" She snatched my phone off the desk and chewed on her bottom lip as she thought.

"I don't know, Mandy. This might be a bad idea." I trailed after her as we moved through the desks. "What if he gets mad and retaliates?"

Mandy snorted, giving me a sideways look. "And what? Tell people that two girls pulled a fast one on him?" She made a disgusted sound in her throat. "He has too much pride. No. He'll run off with his tail between his legs and never darken our doorsteps again." She paused and frowned. "Or well, you know, phones. Whatever. The point is, you need this closure. And this will give you that."

I cocked a brow. "Are you sure you aren't the one who needs closure?"

Her brows shot up to her hairline. "What? Me? No. No way. I'm over him. Way over him. I'm seeing Jacob now. Remember?"

Nodding, I pretended that I believed her. I still thought it was a bad idea, but who knows, maybe it would help me feel better? If I couldn't take my anger out on my dad's killer, then Dean would be the next best thing.

On my way to my next class, Dean caught me in the hallway. He gave me that lopsided grin that used to melt me into a puddle. Now it only made me want to punch him in the face. Still, I put on a smile and tightened my fingers around the strap of my backpack.

"Hey, Dean."

"Hey," he shoved his hands into his pockets and glanced around before shifting over to the side of the hallway. "I got your message."

"Yeah," I began and then swallowed, not sure how to go about this. I wasn't the deceiving type. Playing tricks on people had never been my thing, so even lying to Dean, someone I loathed, was hard to do.

Dean must have thought I was nervous because he reached out and tipped my chin up. "Hey, don't worry. I'm not mad. I promise."

I resisted the urge to snort. He'd been singing a completely different tune a few days ago.

"I know," I turned my head, playing shy. "I just..." I licked my lips and pushed myself to look him in the eyes. If I was going to lie, I was going to do it right. "I miss you, Dean."

"Oh, yeah? I miss you too." He moved a little closer, brushing my hair back over one ear. "What do you say we skip class, and you can start on making it up to me?" He leaned in to kiss me, and I backed up. His expression turned annoyed. "I don't get it, Braxton. You're hot, and then you're cold. What the fuck is going on?"

Taking a deep breath, so I couldn't kick the ass hole in the balls, I shook my head. "No, it's not like that. Just, I can't miss class today. I'm sorry. I just...I missed too much already, and if I miss anymore, I might lose my financial aid." I put a pleading tone to my voice and hoped that Dean wouldn't see right through me.

His features smoothed over, and that easy-going grin was back in place. "Oh, is that all? I understand, baby." He wrapped his hands around my waist and drew me closer. "How about after school?"

"I have to work tonight," I blurted out and then quickly added on, "I mean, I work the overnight shift at the cemetery."

"The cemetery?" Dean frowned, not catching on to what I was saying.

Giving him a shy, but what I hoped was a coy smile, I murmured, "Where I work alone all night long." I trailed my fingers over the front of his polo shirt and bit my bottom lip. "It sure would be nice to have some company. You know what I mean?"

Dean arched one brow and smirked. "Oh, yeah, I do." He rubbed his thumbs between the edge of my shirt and my pants, and I shuddered. He apparently took this as a good thing and went in to kiss me once more.

MY SOUL TO TAKE

Thank all that was holy, the bell rang just then.

"Shit!" I jerked back from him. "I've got to go." I pushed around him and bolted for my class. When I settled in English, Dean texted me.

What time should I come tonight? ;-)

I shot back a response. *10. My boss should be gone by then.*

Edgar didn't stay around that long, trusting me to take care of things as soon as I got there. However, Mandy and I needed time to set up, and I needed to make sure some certain ghosts didn't get in the way.

Dean messaged me back. *Can't wait.*

My stomach rolled. I hated this. Why was I doing this again? Oh, yeah. For Mandy. And I guess a little bit for me. Not to forget all the other girls he probably fucked with too.

I kept telling myself that throughout the rest of the day. I couldn't eat lunch. I was too nervous about that night. When I met Mandy at Bonnie's at the end of the day, I couldn't drink my milkshake either. I stirred the chunky mixture with a massive lump in my throat.

"You better drink up, Brax," Mandy urged me. "You're going to need your strength for tonight."

"Yeah, I know." I huffed a sigh and took a sip to appease her.

Mandy watched me for a long moment and then asked, "You're not having second thoughts, are you?"

"What?" I met her gaze. "No." Yes. "I mean, maybe. I just don't like lying. I'm not good at it. And what are you even going to do to scare him? There are just too many unknowns."

Mandy waved me off. "You worry too much. Leave the scaring to me. And as far as lying, you got him to agree to come, didn't you?"

"Well, yeah."

"Then, you're fine at it." She gave me a thumbs up and slurped a large sip of her shake. "So, tonight. What do you think you're going to wear?"

I shot a look down at what I was wearing now. Jeans and a striped V-neck shirt. "What's wrong with what I have on?"

Mandy laughed, shaking her blonde hair back and forth. "You're not going to convince him that you're sorry in that." She pointed at my clothes. "You need to show a little skin. This is supposed to be a date, right? Then dress like it."

"I don't know." I shifted in my seat, and she gave me a firm look. "Fine. Okay. I'll change when I get home. Which," I glanced at my phone at the time. "I should do now if I'm going to get all dressed up for my fake date in time."

Mandy waved goodbye. I gave her a weak smile.

All the way home and through getting prepped for the date, I had a knot in my stomach. I made myself eat a sandwich before packing my lunch for work. I had tossed the burger from the other day and knew I couldn't stomach something so greasy right now. If I could keep down what I had eaten already at all.

Eventually, it was time for work, and I couldn't delay any longer.

Dean messaged me as I pulled into the driveway of the cemetery.

*Can't wait for tonight. *kissy face**

I walked up to the cemetery gates, my hair curled and bouncing on my shoulders as I walked. I tried to keep my outfit simple but date appropriate. I didn't want Edgar to get suspicious if I showed up dressed to the nines. I'd put on eyeshadows, mascara, and lipstick but kept the rest of my face bare—my earrings, which were little crosses, dangled against the sides of my face. A matching necklace sat in the hollow of my throat, surrounded by the silky cloth of the dark purple halter top I wore. I had put on a pair of my better jeans and ankle boots. I didn't care what Mandy said. I wasn't wearing a skirt in the cemetery in November. I at least had my nice black jacket to cover up my top, so it didn't look so out of place or freeze my nipples off.

Edgar sat behind the desk as I entered the office. His gaze looked up from the papers he was working on and to the watch on his wrist. "Ah, that time already? Where does the time go?"

He gave me a wide grin that I returned with about only a quarter of enthusiasm. If he noticed my attire, he didn't mention it. Not that I expected him to. He was my boss, not my boyfriend. Ew. Visual. Not good.

Shaking my head, I took the keys from Edgar and waved at him as he left.

Alone, at last, I tossed my back on the couch and wiped my hands on my jeans. I was sweating like a pig, and I still had several hours to wait until Dean would get there. Deciding that I wasn't going to be able to concentrate on my homework, I grabbed my flashlight and the keys and headed out the door. Maybe a walk would soothe my nerves.

Chapter 15

I HALF EXPECTED TO get bombarded by the guys the moment I stepped out of the office, but I didn't. It was eerily quiet in the cemetery, and that was saying something.

Brows drawn close together, I walked down the pathway, shining my flashlight in the dim light of the stars and moon. The trees didn't even move in the breeze as I swept the graveyard for my usual ghostly companions.

I kept walking until I heard something. Angling my head to the side, I listened. Was that...water? My eyes widened as I realized that I must be close to the creek everyone kept warning me off of.

As I grew closer, I heard voices. A couple of them I recognized but one I didn't.

"Don't try to stop me. I need to see her," the voice said, desperation in its tone.

"Sir, I appeal to you. Do not do this. You do not know what lies beyond the great veil. It is best not to find out," Shakespeare tried to coherence the other person.

"Yeah, what the brit said," Rooster added on. "You're gonna end up on the bottom side of someone's shoe. You keep acting like a whack ado. No broad is worth that."

I came around the trees to see Rooster and Shakespeare standing around another man, his transparent body clearly labeling him as one of the deceased. They had their hands out to him but not touching him as he inched toward the creek. I stared hard at the stream, wondering what was so special about this spot. Then I saw it. The air wobbled and shimmered in one place above the creek, right behind the man.

What was that?

The ghost wasn't moved by either Rooster or Shakespeare's words. "You don't know her," he said with anger on his face. "She's my everything, and she needs to know. She needs to know I love her."

"I'm sure she does, Tommy." Shakespeare reached out slowly to the other ghost. "She wouldn't come here every day if she didn't."

MY SOUL TO TAKE

Shaking his head profusely, Tommy backed away from them. "No. I need to see her. Be with her. I won't be stuck in this hell hole forever."

Something cracked beneath my booted foot, and all of them turned my way. I held my hands up and froze. As if that would keep them from seeing me.

"Braxton," Shakespeare's eyes skimmed over my form, his lips turning up before frowning. "This isn't a good time."

"Yeah, doll face. Go back to the front. We've got this." Rooster walked toward me as if to usher me back.

Tommy took their distraction as his chance. He spun around and threw himself through the shimmering air. I shouted for them to look, but it was too late. Tommy screamed an agonizing sound before it ended abruptly.

"Shit." Rooster pulled his cigarette from his mouth. "There goes another one."

"What the hell is going on?" I gaped, scrambling closer to them. "Why did that guy just...did he just die? Like really die die?"

"Yes, I fear so." Shakespeare blew out a breath and rubbed over his face. I wondered if it was just habit since ghosts couldn't or didn't need to breathe. I guess some things like even breathing were hard habits to break.

I moved closer to the creek, my eyes on the rippling air. "Why would he go through there if he knew he was going to die?"

"He didn't, doll." Rooster shrugged his leather jacket up further on his shoulders. "He was trying to get out."

"Get out?" I frowned, turning away from the space to look at him. "From where?"

Rooster huffed a laugh. "The cemetery, sweetheart. The only place we got to get out of." He held his arms out wide and turned in a circle. "We're trapped here—no coming. No going. Just waiting until the end. Whenever that is."

"Only God knows our true design of mortal man."

I rolled my eyes over to Shakespeare. "Really? You're dead. Your design is already over."

"Not for all of us," Rooster answered. "Not for ghosts. We still have something to do. Some unfinished business that's keeping us here."

Glancing between the two of them, I frowned. "Then why don't you do it and move on?"

Ben barked a laugh. "Oh, 'twould it be so of ease. The blind man cannot walk the path he cannot see."

My brows furrowed as I tried to decipher Ben's words. "You mean, you don't know what your unfinished business is?"

Rooster clicked his tongue and pointed a finger gun at me. "You got it, babycakes."

I ignored his blatant attempt to annoy me with all the pet names. "Okay, so find out your unfinished business, and then what?" I crossed my arms over my chest, jerking my head toward the rippling air. "That still doesn't explain this."

"We can't leave." Champ or rather Rider appeared from the trees. I forced the anger that billowed up inside of me down so I could hear what he had to say. "Even if we know our unfinished business, we can't go anywhere to do it. We're stuck here with our bodies. The only way out of here is to cross through here." He nodded behind me.

"But it killed that guy." My nose scrunched up as I added on, "Again."

"Precisely," Ben placed a hand on his hip, the other pointing at the ripple. "To cross the barrier, thou must be pure of intentions, and no earthling is so pure."

"So, even if you know your unfinished business, you can't complete it to move on unless you get out of the cemetery, but you can't get out of the cemetery unless you go through the swirly portal of death and hope that your heart is pure?" I grabbed the sides of my head and shook it slightly. "Why is the afterlife so confusing?"

Rooster shrugged. "Beats the hell outta me. I just work here. I don't run the joint."

"Braxton!"

My head turned toward the sound of my name. Damn. Mandy was here already?

"Who's that?" Rider asked, apparently not afraid I would wallop him.

I shot him a look. "My friend. And I'm still not done with you."

"Never said otherwise," Rider answered back, this time with a bit more backbone to his words. I had a feeling he wouldn't just let me wail on him like before.

Huffing my annoyance, I started back to the front of the cemetery where Mandy's voice was coming from. To my increasing irritation, I had three ghosts tailing after me the whole way.

I lowered my voice and scowled over my shoulder, "You guys don't have to follow me everywhere."

"What else are we going to do?" Rider asked, his lip ticking up at the sides.

So much for his good boy routine. "I don't know. And I don't care. I just don't need you tagging along and making me look insane."

Rooster snorted a laugh.

Unfortunately, my words did nothing to deter them from following me like three creepy shadows.

I tried my best to ignore them and walked up to Mandy, who was just a second away from peeing herself. "Hey."

Mandy screamed, jumping in place.

"Jesus," I wiggled a finger in my ear and winced. "I kind of need my eardrums Mandy. Fuck."

"Oops." Mandy giggled, clinging her bag to her chest. "This place is just so freaking creepy. I don't know how you stand it."

I shrugged. "It's not so bad." I forced myself not to look at the ghosts who were hanging on to our every word. "So, what's in the bag?"

Mandy stopped shaking in her designer boots and held her bag out with a grin. "Oh, you're gonna love this. I found some really scary stuff at the costume store." She pulled a long white face with black eyes out along with a flowing black cloak. "And look," she pushed something on the mask, and it laughed a haunting sound. "Pretty terrifying, huh?"

"Uh, yeah." I gave her two thumbs up. If Dean was scared by this, he was a bigger douche nozzle than I thought he was.

"So, where are you going to take him on your date? I want to figure out where I'm going to hang out." She smoothed her hands over her costume, quite proud of her find.

"Date?" Rooster asked, his gaze sliding over my form once more. "You have a date?"

"Yep, I have a date. Here in the cemetery," I answered them, getting a strange look from Mandy.

"Yeah, I know. Where do you want to do it?" Mandy cocked her head to the side. "Are you sure you're okay to do this? We can call it off if you want."

Before I could answer her, Rider asked, "You have a date with her? And you brought her to the cemetery?"

Rooster whistled, eyes on the costume. "Kinky."

Ben seemed utterly flummoxed by the whole situation. His eyes kept going from me to Mandy and back.

Gritting my jaw, I focused on Mandy. "My date with Dean. A guy from school." Mandy's eyes narrowed on me, and I quickly changed my tone. Clearing my throat, I gestured over to a set of trees. "I figured we could do it over there. It has plenty of coverage for you and gives Dean a straight shot out of the cemetery when he turns tail and runs."

"Wait a second now." Rooster gaffed, smacking his leg with a hand. "You mean to scare the bejeezus out of some poor sap. Is that what gals do on dates nowadays?" He huffed a laugh. "Man, and here I was taking them to lovers' lane for a little necking."

My eyes rolled over to Rooster, but I didn't answer him. To Mandy, I said, "You can get changed in the office. Dean will be here in about an hour."

"Got it." Mandy gathered her things and skipped to the office with a big smile on her lips.

When she was gone, I turned to the guys, my hands on my hips. "Listen, Mandy and I have plans tonight. Plans that don't include you three. So, you can do what you do best and disappear."

For once, they actually listened to me.

Flipping my curls over my jacket neck, I prepared myself for what would be a challenging and hopefully entertaining night.

Chapter 16

I HAD TO REAPPLY my deodorant twice before Dean finally showed up for our date. Mandy was already in position complaining about it being hotter than Hades' butthole inside the mask she bought when Dean's Hummer pulled up to the cemetery gates.

Rubbing my hands on my jeans, I plastered a smile on my face. "You came."

Dean shut the door of his ugly ass yellow Hummer and smirked. "You thought I wouldn't?"

Mandy and I had decided I should play the shy repentant façade. It would help me if I fumbled with my lies. God knew I would need all the help I could get.

MY SOUL TO TAKE

"This is the gentleman you have damned to be brought to his knees by your trickery?" Ben appeared by my side, his eyes looking over Dean with his nose in the air.

I didn't answer Ben, plastering a coy grin on my lips for Dean. "Well, I don't know. I thought maybe you wouldn't..." I trailed off and shrugged, allowing him to fill in the blanks for himself.

Dean brushed his thumb across his lower lip and chuckled to himself. "No, no. I do. I mean, I'm glad you wanted to go out." He paused and glanced around the graveyard. "I'm surprised you would want to meet here, though. I'd expect you to want to go somewhere more..." he sucked his teeth, and a sleazy grin slid up his face. "Private."

I sashayed up to Dean and placed a hand on his chest, dipping my head as I stroked his chest. "It is private." I giggled and met his gaze. "Not unless you think ghosts are going to be watching us?"

He let out a nervous chuckle. "Nah, I guess not."

"Come on," I slid my hand into his and led him deeper into the cemetery.

Ben watched us with disapproval on his face. I ignored him.

"Do you have a flashlight? I can't see a damn thing." Dean cried out in pain. "Ouch. Damn it."

I pulled my flashlight out of my back pocket and held it out. "Oops, sorry. I guess I forgot about it with...you know." I ducked my head, glancing up at him from beneath my lashes. I hoped the moonlight was enough for him to see what I was doing. I'd hate all my hard work to be wasted because he couldn't see it.

I didn't have to worry, though. Dean licked his lips and wrapped an arm around my waist, pulling me close. "Oh, don't worry. I'm not that breakable."

Resisting the urge to snort and pull away, I muttered to myself, "We'll see about that."

"What?" Dean glanced down at me. "Did you say something?"

I giggled and brushed my hair behind my ear. "Just talking to myself."

"There's no reason to be nervous, Braxton." Dean rubbed my waist with his hand. "I like you. I really do."

Pulling my lower lip between my teeth, I worried it as if I were having a hard time saying the next words, "I really like you too, Dean."

He leaned down, and I froze. Dean's lips brushed mine, and I forced myself to relax. If I pushed him away now, then it would be all over. This would be all for nothing.

So, I let the bastard kiss me. His breath smelled like nachos, and he used far too much tongue. I felt like I was drowning in jalapeno spit.

Pulling away, I resisted the urge to wipe my mouth and maybe gargle with pure acid as I tugged on his hand. "Come on, I have a spot all picked out for us."

"Oh, you do, do you?" Dean followed after me like a puppy dog with a treat. I guess the metaphor wasn't too far behind, except, in this case, I was the treat.

We came upon the place under the trees where I had laid out a picnic blanket. There was a cooler with a few beers in it and a couple of throw pillows I'd taken from the office. The moon came through the trees ever so slightly to give it a twilight effect.

"You did all this for me?" Dean pulled me close once more, kissing me softly and then more forcefully. When we had to part to breathe, I took my chance to speak. God knew when he'd let me do that again.

"Why don't we sit down and get more comfortable?" I suggested. Dean did so without complaint, and I busied myself getting us a beer. "Drink?"

"Thanks." Dean took the bottle and twisted off the top.

"This is your idea of a date, doll face?" Rooster propped up against a nearby tree. "You ain't been treated right if you think this is a ball." He shifted his cigarette from one side of his mouth to the other and stared down at me. "Now, I could show you a good time. You'll be praying so hard the angels themselves will weep."

I choked on some of the beer. Coughing, I patted at my chest, trying to get the liquid out of my windpipe. Dean sat up and patted me on the back hard. So hard that I thought I might end up with a red mark on my back for hours later.

"You okay?"

"Yeah," I croaked. "Wrong pipe is all."

Dean nodded and went back to drinking his beer. He finished it off before I'd even gotten halfway through mine and turned his attention back to me. Wrapping his arms around my waist, he began to kiss along my neck in small stinging bites. Whoever thought this was a turn on could go suck a big one. Pain for pleasure was so not my thing.

Where the hell was Mandy?

Dean lifted his head from my neck. "Woah, what's with all the fog?"

I sat up and twisted around to where he was looking. There was indeed a roll of fog coming in. What else did Mandy have in that bag of tricks of hers?

"It's alright," I told him, sliding my hand up beneath his shirt. "It's kind of romantic, don't you think?"

Dean gave me an unusual look before his eyes went back to the fog. They widened a second later. "Did you see that?"

I frowned, pretending to squint. "See what?"

"I think someone's out there." Dean shifted away from me and stared out into the trees.

I scrambled to my feet, shifting from one foot to the other. "They better not be. I'll have to call the cops and Edgar if they are, and then our whole evening is ruined."

Dean's head whipped up at that, and he grabbed my hand in his. "Don't worry, baby. I'm sure it's nothing. Just an animal."

I pursed my lips and squeezed his hand tight. "Are you sure?"

"Completely." He bobbed his head, but he was so talking out of his ass.

A splinter of wood made me jump for real, and I grabbed onto Dean. "What was that? Can you go check Dean? Please?"

Dean's face was a mixture of apprehension and the need to get laid. His hand slid over my ass as he stared out into the dark. I forced myself not to dropkick the pervert in the nuts reminding myself this was the plan.

Finally, Dean held his hand out. "Give me the flashlight. You stay here. I'll find this little fucker, and then we can get back to the real fun." He gave me a lecherous grin, which I pretended melted my panties when really it made me want to gag.

Mandy had better be ready. We would only get one shot at this, and I didn't want to miss it because she was texting.

I watched Dean as he crept into the trees, the flashlight doing him no good with all the fog floating around. I'd have to ask Mandy how much she spent on this whole thing cause really, that much fog had to cost a pretty penny.

Dean jumped and startled at every sound, and it took everything in me not to giggle at his expense. I was supposed to be scared, not laughing like a schoolgirl. When another crack in the trees made him spin around in place the flashlight up like a weapon, I snorted and then coughed, trying to cover my slip up.

"You okay, baby?" Dean called back to me.

"Please hurry, Dean. I'm so worried."

After a few moments, Dean started back to me. "Whatever it was is gone now. Why don't we-"

Right then, Mandy's ghostfaced costume appeared in the smoke, her black body looking as if she were floating through the air. She had a plastic stage dagger in one hand with fake blood dripping from it.

I let out a petrified scream that would have won me an academy award had we been in a movie as I pointed behind him. To my utter delight, Dean turned slowly around, dropped the flashlight, too shocked to hold on to it. He didn't scream as well as I did, but he did let out a shout and screamed, "Fuck this," before bolting for the cemetery gates.

His Hummer had peeled out of the driveway before I could even chase after him to really bring it home.

"Well?" Mandy stopped beside me, pulling her mask off. "Think it worked?"

I shrugged. "I guess we'll see. But if I was him, I wouldn't want anyone to know what happened here tonight when faced with a real ghost."

"That poor bastard," Rooster appeared nearby, shaking his head. "You've gone and traumatized him for life. Just wrong."

"He deserved it," Mandy said as if answering Rooster. "It might not stop him from messing with other girls, but at least he'll steer clear of you now."

"Yeah, I hope so," I replied back, then bust out laughing. "Did you see his face?"

Mandy joined my laughter. We both spent the next hour replaying the events of Dean's humiliation until we were rolling on the ground giggling with tears down our faces and the three ghosts watched us with disbelief. Who said haunting was just for the undead?

Chapter 17

WHEN I WOKE THE next evening, I felt lighter. I didn't expect scaring the crap out of Dean would make me feel...feel so alive. But it did.

I even sang in the shower, which I hadn't done since before Dad died. My hips wiggled from side to side while I dried off with a towel. I hummed a tune to myself as I got dressed for the day, picking out a skirt with thick stockings and a clingy top. Usually, I wouldn't bother getting all dressed up, but today, today was special.

Skipping down the stairs, I pulled cheese and butter from the fridge and went about making my dad's famous grilled cheese. The secret ingredient? Sautéed onions. Weird for grilled cheese, I know, but so tasty you'd sell your soul for another one. I hadn't had the heart to make one since he passed. He didn't get to have it, so why should I?

It was a new day. A new chapter. Which called for a celebration.

I danced around the kitchen working on my meal, so consumed by my happiness, I almost didn't hear my phone ringing. Putting my plate down, I picked it up and saw Mandy was calling. "Hey, Mandy. Are you flying on cloud nine like I am?"

"Braxton, we've got a problem." There was a panic in her voice that made me frown.

"What's wrong?"

"He knows," her voice went to a low whisper. "Dean knows we screwed with him. I don't know how, but he does."

I shifted the phone from one ear to the other, my shoulder hunched over it. "What do you mean he knows? We didn't tell anyone. I didn't." I paused, and then my jaw tightened. "Mandy...who did you tell?"

Mandy didn't answer.

"Damn it, Mandy! Who did you tell?"

Mandy sucked in a sharp breath. "Jacob. I told Jacob, okay?"

"Fucking hell." I slammed my hand down on the counter, making the plate bounce. "You're the one who wanted to do this, and now you've gone and screwed it up."

"I'm sorry, okay. I didn't think he'd go and tell anyone." Mandy cried into the phone big, huge wailing sobs.

I dropped my head down and let out a long breath. "Look, it's done. It's over. What's Dean going to do? Tell on us? Just chill out and kick Jacob's ass for being such a tattletale."

Mandy laughed through her tears. "Yeah, okay. Be careful, okay?"

"I will." I hung up and sighed. Leaning over the island, I stared at the wood for a long moment. My eyes slid over to the grilled cheese and glared at it. I picked up the plate and stomped over to the trash, dumping the sandwich inside it before tossing the plate in the sink. It broke. Fuck it.

I made my lunch and headed out to my dad's car. I chucked my bag into the passenger side and slammed the door shut. There was no singing on the way to work. No blasting the radio. I half expected to get pulled over for how fast I was booking it to the cemetery.

To my relief, Dean wasn't waiting for me at the cemetery. Unfortunately, three ghosts were waiting for me right inside the gates.

"I don't want to hear it, guys." I walked past them as fast as I could, not wanting to deal with them today.

"Do not take ire with us. We only wish to warn you," Ben called after me.

MY SOUL TO TAKE

I stopped and turned back to them. "Warn me about what?"

"That the candy-ass you two ladies tried to spook last night," Rooster continued, taking a few steps toward me.

"Yeah?" I crossed my arms over my chest, staring him down. What about him?"

"He came back today. Looking for you, doll face." Rooster pulled the cigarette from his mouth and eyeballed me. "And he looked ready to blow his top."

I snorted and tried to walk away. "Don't worry about Dean. I can handle him."

"You say that," Champ cut me off, "but I know guys like him. Hell, my fraternity was filled to the brim with them. They think everyone owes them something. And he will definitely be coming to collect now."

My heart shuddered at his words. I swallowed the lump in my throat and forced a confident smile. "I'm touched by your concern, but I'll be fine."

Spinning on my heels, I went into the office. Edgar had already left, something about an appointment. I guess when you were in charge, you could come and go whenever you wanted. I sighed and threw my bag down. There was no way I was going to get any homework done today.

I glanced at my phone. Still, I hadn't gotten a single call or text from Dean. I didn't know if that was a good thing or a bad thing. I was hoping good. Maybe he was too embarrassed and wouldn't mess with me.

The sound of glass breaking jerked my head up. What the hell? There wasn't any glass out there to break. Except...

Shit.

I raced out of the office and darted for the gate. "What the fuck are you doing, you psycho?" I screamed at Dean, standing with a sledgehammer over my dad's precious convertible.

Dean smirked at me, lifting the hammer up. "This is for leading me on, bitch." He slammed the hammer down on the side view mirror, knocking it off. Each hit of the hammer gutted me to the core. While I wanted to rush out there and stop him, I wasn't stupid. No way was I putting myself next to a pissed off Dean when he was wielding a sledgehammer.

"Man, he's pissed." Champ appeared at my side, whistling as he rocked on his heels.

"You know, I liked you better when you were just Champ," I told him before stomping closer to the gate. "I'm calling the cops, Dean. You won't get away with this."

Dean scoffed. "No, you won't. Then I'd have to tell them what you did to me."

"We played a prank, Dean," I snapped. "I didn't destroy your property. That's my dad's car, you asshole."

MY SOUL TO TAKE

Grinning maliciously, Dean said, "Well, now it's scrap metal."

I growled, pulling my phone out and dialing the cops. "Yeah, I'd like to report a crime in progress."

"You aren't seriously calling the cops on me, Braxton? After you humiliated me?" Dean lowered the hammer and glared at me. "You're going to regret this, you teasing whore."

Dean got into his ugly yellow Hummer and peeled out of the driveway.

"Ma'am, ma'am, are you still there?" The emergency operator asked.

"Yeah, I'm still here."

"Is the perpetrator still there?"

Rooster leaned against the gate and chuckled, shaking his head. "Dollface, you have really stepped in it this time."

"What would you know about it?" I snapped at him and then answered the operator's startled question. "No, not you. And no, he left. Can someone come down here and check it out? I need a police report for my insurance."

"Of course, someone will be out there shortly. Where are you located?"

I rattled off the address for the cemetery and hung up the phone. "Why did it have to be my dad's car? Damn it."

"Would you rather it have been you?" Champ arched a brow at me.

I shot him a look. "Of course not. Just..." I sighed. "This was his baby. Besides me, anyway, I'd hate to think he was looking down on me and seeing how it was getting treated."

Ben placed a hand on my shoulder. "Your father would be a sorry fellow indeed to place his possessions above his own flesh and blood."

"I know. And he wouldn't. Still, fuck." I shook my head and sat on a bench near the path and waited for the police.

When they arrived, I spent the next hour explaining what had happened and who had done it. They warned me to keep an eye out for him in case he came back.

"Guys like that, don't just let things go," the police officer warned me. "Are you sure you don't want someone to stay until you go home?"

I shook my head. "No, it'll be alright. I have a friend coming."

The police left, leaving me alone with the ghosts.

"Why did you tell them your friend was coming?" Champ asked.

"Because she is when my shift is over," I told him as I walked into the office. I closed and locked the door behind me. "Besides, I doubt he'll be back. He wouldn't be stupid enough to attack me after the cops were just here."

"I wouldn't be so sure about that, babe." Rooster pointed a finger at me. "That guy definitely had a few loose screws if you know what I'm sayin'."

"Never fear, my lady." Ben bowed at the waist. "We will protect you if it should come to a brawl."

"Pfft. And do what? Annoy him to death? He can't even see you?" I flopped down on the couch and turned on the television.

"We can touch others if we focus enough," Champ reminded me.

I shook my head. "You can't protect me forever. I won't be here all the time, and you can't follow me home. So, don't make promises you can't keep."

The night went by slowly. Like stuck in a time loop slow. I was never more grateful for the sun to come up that Sunday morning than today.

"Are you sure you're goin' to be okay, doll?" Rooster shifted from foot to foot, rolling his cigarette from one side of his mouth to the other.

"I'll be fine," I reassured him. A horn honked outside. "That'll be Mandy. I'll see you tonight."

Leaving the office, I walked quickly to the gate and what was left of my dad's beautiful car. It probably still ran, but It wasn't drivable until the mechanic could look at it. A tow truck was going to come by sometime today and get it. I made them wait until morning so they wouldn't charge me up the ass.

"Oh, Braxton," Mandy gaped at my car as I climbed into the passenger seat. "I'm so sorry."

"Yeah, well," I huffed a long breath. "It's just a car."

"But it was your dad's."

I turned my face out toward the window. "Yeah. It was."

The drive to the house was quiet. Mandy tried to make conversation, but she stopped trying to talk to me when I didn't respond.

I slammed the car door shut behind me once we were parked in the driveway at my house.

Mandy called out after me, but I ignored her, set on getting inside.

Dropping my bag at the back door, I dropped my car keys on the counter and raced up the stairs. I just wanted this day to be over.

Going into the bathroom, I brushed my teeth and took care of business. I walked to my dresser and pulled out a long t-shirt for bed. In the middle of pulling the shirt over my head, a slam from downstairs sounded.

I jerked the shirt on completely and frowned. "Mandy? Is that you?" I called out into the hallway. When there wasn't an answer, I grabbed my pepper spray from my nightstand and then crept down the stairs.

Walking into the kitchen, I found the back door wide open but no one in sight. I shook my head as I closed the door and locked it. "Just the wind, Braxton. Jesus, you're losing your mind."

I turned around, more than ready to go to bed.

"Not yet, but you will." My eyes jerked over to the voice.

"Dean?" I gaped at him. "What the hell are you doing in my house? Get out of here."

Eyes hard, they slid over my pantless legs, and his lips curled up into an evil grin. "Not until I get payment for the humiliation you and your bitch friend put me through."

I stared at him for a long second before making a run for the stairs. If I could get upstairs, I could get to my cell phone and call the cops. My pepper spray was tight in my fist, but it wouldn't do me any good until Dean was right up on me.

"Oh no, you don't." Dean chased after me.

I screamed, hoping one of my neighbors would hear the commotion and call the cops for me. My foot went out from under me as I hit the stairs. I put my hand out to brace myself, dropping the pepper spray. It bounced on the stairs and rolled away, leaving me defenseless with Dean.

"Let me go," I shouted, shoving and kicking at him. My fist hit him in the face, and for a brief second, I was free. I scrambled for the pepper spray. Arms wrapped tightly around me as my hand clenched the canister in my palm.

"Come on, Braxton. We were having fun before." Dean hissed in my ear, grabbing at the edge of my shirt. "If you don't fight, you might even like it."

"Doubtful, you limp dick freak." I swung my head back, but Dean must have expected it, and all I hit was air.

One moment Dean was holding me, and the next, he was flying across the room. I spun around, my pepper spray up and ready to hit him in the face. What I saw were three ghosts wailing on Dean. Well, except for Rooster. Every other of his punches seemed to be just going right through Dean.

I stayed back in the corner watching them beat on Dean and did nothing to stop them. I didn't know if they killed him or not, and at that moment I really didn't care. They'd come for me. These three ghosts who didn't know me from Eve, saved me.

When it was clear Dean wasn't getting up again, they turned to me. Tears slid down my face as I sank down on the floor in a mixture of horror and relief.

"My lady, did this curd injure you?" Ben knelt before me, brushing his finger across my cheek. "My apologies for our late arrival."

"No," I hiccupped, shaking my head. "He didn't get the chance."

"Good." Champ held a hand out to me, lifting me to my feet. "You probably should call the cops before he wakes up."

I nodded numbly and stumbled up the stairs, my legs having trouble remembering how to work. After I called the cops, I returned to the living room and the three ghosts. "How...how did you know?" I gaped at them, unable to believe that they were really standing before me.

"The bastard came back to the cemetery right after you left," Champ explained, giving Dean one more kick to the side. "We knew he'd likely come to your house next."

"But how'd you get here?"

Ben gave me a meaningful look.

I shook my head, and a short laugh escaped. "No way. No way you guys threatened your own lives to save me." My gaze moved across each one of their transparent faces. Rooster smirked, his cigarette shifting from one side of his mouth to the other. Champ shrugged an aw-shucks kind of gesture.

Ben was the only one who had the balls to say anything for themselves. "What can we say to ease the trepidation in your heart, Braxton? We simply could not imagine this fair world without your lovely visage in it."

"Yeah, what he said," Rooster jerked his chin toward Ben.

I swallowed hard, my eyes burning. "That's not possible. I thought you had to be pure of intentions to cross?"

Champ shoved his hands into his pockets. "At that moment, all of us wanted nothing more than to save you." He scratched behind his ear. "I guess that was enough."

I sank down on the couch and shook my head. It was just too mind-blowing. How? Why? I hadn't exactly been nice to them. I guess they were better humans than me, even dead.

"I don't know how to thank you." I licked my lips and dragged my hands through my hair. "You guys saved my life. If it hadn't been for you..." I trailed off, trying not to imagine what Dean would have done to me. The rage on his face. I never imagined Dean would go so ballistic about a little prank. I should have known, though. He was always just one wrong word away from being a homicidal maniac. It was our own damn fault. Mine and Mandy's. Except I was the one he came after—the one he blamed. No, I owed the guys more than just my life.

Red and blue cop lights filled the windows, signaling the Cavalry had come. I stared down at the asshole on the ground, still knocked out, blood dripping from his nose, and made a decision.

Standing, I placed my hands on my hips and smiled. "I know what I'm going to do to repay you."

"Oh, I know a few ways, baby girl." Rooster wagged his eyebrows at me.

Champ smacked Rooster on the back of the head with a scowl.

"No," I said flatly. There was a knock on my front door, telling me my time was almost up and the night long explanation of what happened would start. Walking toward the door, I said over my shoulder, "I'm going to help you find your unfinished business."

They saved me. I'd save them. After all, it was the least I could do.

Chapter 18

A month later...

A COOL BREEZE BRUSHED against my cheek. I shivered and pulled the covers tighter around me.

"Dollface," a sing-song voice called in my ear before the cold air found my toes. "Dollface, you're gonna be late."

I groaned and wiggled my toes deeper into the blankets. "Five more minutes."

Rooster chuckled beside me. "You always say that. We both know you're telling tall tales. So, why don't ya save yourself the scramble and wake up? We have a surprise for you."

"A surprise?" I asked, sitting straight up in bed.

Rooster laughed at me.

"What?" I touched my hair. "Do I have bed head?"

Shaking his head, he pulled the cigarette from between his lips. "Nah. You're gorgeous as always."

I pursed my lips, not sure I believed him. Still, I swung my legs out of bed, acutely aware of Rooster's eyes on my bare legs beneath my long t-shirt.

When the guys first moved in with me, I'd been skittish about the whole sleeping in just a shirt and underwear like I usually did. Still, after a few weeks, it seemed stupid to change what made me comfortable for a few ghosts. Besides, I'd be lying if I said I didn't enjoy the attention.

Smirking at Rooster as I made my way to the bathroom, my hips swayed a bit more than usual.

Rooster cleared his throat. "I'm going to...uh...wait out in the hallway for you."

I arched a brow at him. For such a flirt, Rooster sure acted the gentleman when faced with the female body. It was kind of cute.

When I got to the bathroom, I scowled at my reflection—that little liar. My hair resembled a bees nest, and there was no way I would be able to get a brush through it without wetting it first.

Sighing, I hopped in the shower. Doing a quick condition and rinse, I wrapped my hair in a towel and another around my body and walked back into my room.

"Braxton, you awake?" Champ's head poked through my bedroom door, and I let out a surprised, "eep," my hand going to the top of my towel.

"Champ!"

Champ's eyes scanned over me before his face grew red, and he ducked back out with a muttered apology.

"Ugh. What'd I say about knocking first?" I called through the bedroom door while hurrying to find my clothing. One negative about living with ghosts was they had no sense of privacy.

"Hey, you let Rooster just walk in." He countered, sticking his head back through with his eyes closed.

"That's because he hasn't mastered the knock yet." I threw my towel at his head, which went straight through him and hit the door. "You have no excuse."

"Fine. Whatever," Champ pouted. "Just hurry up. It's getting cold."

I frowned. "What's getting cold?"

When Champ didn't answer me, I scrambled into my clothes, rushing out the door and into the hallway where all the ghosts had conveniently disappeared from.

MY SOUL TO TAKE

Twisting my lips to one side, I moved down the hallway and toward the stairs. The scent of bacon wafted through the air, and I picked up the pace.

Bounding down the stairs, I raced into the kitchen, expecting to find a mess or at least something on fire. Instead, I found three smug ghosts standing at the island.

"What's all this?" I slid my eyes over the countertop. Pancakes, waffles, eggs, a bowl of sliced mixed fruit, and of course, bacon all lined the countertop.

"It's your birthday breakfast, of course." Champ grinned from ear to ear, entirely too pleased with himself.

"Did you do all this?" I asked Champ, grabbing the back of a chair to sit down.

Ben pulled the chair out for me with a bow. "Not all of it." He offered me his hand, and I giggled, allowing him to help me into my seat. Ben pushed me up to the bar and picked up my hand. "May your days be full of mirth, and shall your beauty only increase with age." He placed a cool kiss against the back of my hand.

I rolled my eyes. "Shakespeare, must you always sound like your namesake?"

Ben spit to the side. "Namesake? Willy wishes he were as poetic as I. And when will you call me by my God-given name?"

I picked up a strawberry and bit into it, intentionally making full eye contact. His eyes dipped to my lips, and I smiled. "When you earn it. Besides, I could call you Brit like Rooster?"

Rooster puffed up his chest and gave Ben a Cheshire smile.

"Lord Almighty save me from my loved ones, for they will be the death of me." Ben sighed and combed a hand through his brown hair. His words were a complaint, but his eyes were bright with what I could only call joy.

Just then, the back-kitchen door swung open, and Aunt Christine appeared, stomping her feet on the welcome mat and closing her umbrella. "Oh, Braxton. I'm so sorry, I'm late." She moved her hair back and forth, sprinkling water all around her. She busied herself, putting her purse up and hanging her umbrella as she spoke, not seeing the layout in front of me right away. "And on your birthday. I hope you aren't feeling too down. I know you really wanted your dad here, but you'll just have to settle- oh!" Her eyes finally landed on the spread of food on the counter, her mouth falling open in surprise. "Wow, did you do all this?"

I smiled. "No, a few friends stopped by to wish me a happy birthday."

Aunt Christine chuckled as she plucked a piece of bacon from a plate. Biting into it, she chewed while waving the remaining bacon at me. "And here I was feeling guilty that I wouldn't be here before you woke up. But you're doing just fine, aren't you?"

My gaze slid to the guys who tried their best to stay out of the rampaging disposal that was my Aunt Christine. A small secretive smile crept up my lips. "Yeah, I guess I'm going to be just fine."

About the Author

Erin Bedford is an otaku, recovering coffee addict, and Legend of Zelda fanatic. Her brain is so full of stories that need to be told that she must get them out or explode into a million screaming chibis. Obsessed with fairy tales and bad boys, she hasn't found a story she can't twist to match her deviant mind full of innuendos, snarky humor, and dream guys.

On the outside, she's a work from home mom and bookbinger. One the inside, she's a thirteen-year-old boy screaming to get out and tell you the pervy joke they found online. As an ex-computer programmer, she dreams of one day combining her love for writing and college credits to make the ultimate video game!

Until then, when she's not writing, Erin is devouring as many books as possible on her quest to have the biggest book gut of all time. She's written over thirty books, ranging from paranormal romance, urban fantasy, and even scifi romance.

Come chat me up!
www.erinbedford.com
Facebook.com/erinrbedford
twitter.com/erin_bedford

Made in the USA
Coppell, TX
12 May 2021